POINTS OF THE COMPASS

"Lovers" by Hrant M. Keshishian

POINTS OF THE COMPASS

Stories by
SAHAR TAWFIQ

*Translated from the Arabic
and with an Introduction and Notes by*
MARILYN BOOTH

THE UNIVERSITY OF ARKANSAS PRESS
Fayetteville 1995

99   98   97   96   95   5   4   3   2   1

Designed by Gail Carter

*Text illustrations are modifications of artwork
    by Hrant M. Keshishian*

Library of Congress Cataloging-in-Publication Data
Tawfīq, Sahar, 1951–
    [Short stories. English. Selections]
    Points of the compass / stories by Sahar Tawfīq ;
translated from the Arabic and with an introduction
and notes by Marilyn Booth.
        p.   cm.
    ISBN 1-55728-385-0 (alk. paper). —
    ISBN 1-55728-384-2 (pbk. : alk. paper)
    I. Booth, Marilyn. II. Title.
PJ7864.A478A6   1995
782'.736—dc20   95-17242
                                  CIP

For Islam and Muhammad,
Paul and Carrie

S. T. & M. B.

ACKNOWLEDGMENTS

I am grateful for the help and encouragement I've received over the course of this project. The enthusiasm and friendship of the author of these stories has been paramount. For memorable and reposeful days in al-Haram, I thank Sahar Tawfiq, Adel al-Sharqawi, and their sons, Islam and Muhammad. For her ready advice and interest, I want to thank Carol Bardenstein. For generous help with sources, I thank Ann Macy Roth. For reading parts of the manuscript, I thank Carol Bardenstein, Eren Giray, Carol Spindel, and John Swanson. Hrant Keshishian took the initiative to produce art specially for this collection, a work of friendship that Sahar and I cannot sufficiently acknowledge. I'm grateful to Marsha Pripstein-Posusney for carrying that precious artwork across the seas. For time, given with understanding, I thank Ken Cuno.

Marilyn Booth
Urbana, Illinois
November 1994

CONTENTS

INTRODUCTION

Sahar Tawfiq's stories are marked by the migrations that have touched the lives of thousands of Egyptians, today and throughout the past—from the new city to the old, from the field to the city, east to west across the Nile, north to south in search of the sacred river's source, away from home, in search of home. These are journeys by foot and in dreams and through tales that are told. In "Nothing Bounds the Wide, Wide Road," a young city woman restlessly walks, looking for her own life. The forced mass exodus and resettlement of Upper Egypt's Nubian population after the construction of the Aswan High Dam and the more recent movement of families from the narrow Nile strip to newly built-up desert areas because they cannot find housing or employment are both suggested if not referenced in "That the Sun May Sink." "Points of the Compass" portrays the mythic journeys along and across the Nile. In the recent "The Time That Is Not This," characters search for another reality marked out in spaces and boundaries and strides. Tawfiq's characters are constituted in their departures and arrivals and the journeys in between. Through their spatial movement, they question notions of settled identities and discrete communities, and they probe the role of memory, both individual and collective.

Sahar Tawfiq is one of a number of outstanding contemporary Egyptian fiction writers who have tackled this postmodern sense of dislocation. Her writing draws on some of the most oft-traveled trajectories that contemporary writers of fiction in Arabic have marked out. Yet in its blurring of the generic identities of fiction and prose poetry and with its particular exploitation of myth and folklore, Tawfiq's voice is distinctive.

This introduction presents a map of these eight translated stories, one that indicates some of their features and directions and situates them within contemporary Egyptian writing; it is not a full analytical treatment. However, I shall discuss "Points of the Compass" at some length because it is a complex rendering of ancient Egyptian mythology and more recent lore, some indication of which is helpful to an appreciation of the story.[1]

· · ·

Tawfiq's writing echoes that landmark work of fiction, Sun`allah Ibrahim's novella *Tilka al-ra'iha* (1966).[2] This short work generated controversy and excitement not only for its explicit autoerotic references but also because of its unrelenting exploitation of strategies that had already begun to appear, if less starkly, in modern Arabic fiction: an utterly estranged point of view, a concentration on the minute and unvarnished details of the everyday in the absence of any meaning that might be less fragmented, and the narrator's abrupt shifts from a flat narration of the skeleton of daily life to fleshier mental musings.

Tawfiq's protagonist is often a lone woman whose external movements are documented sparely and dispassionately, either in the third or the first person, but whom we also see through interspersed interior monologues and terse conversations with one or two others. These others are usually a friend or a lover ("Moments of Walking in Darkness and Sleep, Conversation and Wakefulness," "Nothing Bounds the Wide, Wide Road"),[3] but may also be neighborhood folk not known to the central character by name, whose presence creates a false sense of stable community and history ("Visiting the Old City").

Rather than glorying in her solitude, however, Tawfiq's protagonist reaches out, seeking connection while constantly reaffirming its ephemerality. Enumerating the dangers of expecting stable emotional connection to others and haphazardly attempting or mocking the games that love demands, she finds it impossible to reject this connection wholly. She travels back and forth or wanders without a destination, alienated from home and at the same time searching for it, unable to play comfortably the social role expected of her. While Tawfiq's characters may inhabit the same world that Sun'allah Ibrahim's protagonists wander through, hers experience it and shape it differently, as the differential effects of social gender shadow them.

Like many feminists across the globe (and contrary to many others), Tawfiq links the biological process of reproduction and the related socially defined roles of women to an ethos of caring. In some of her stories, the speaking voice defines an identity through maternal caring and the pain it may bring. This is not, of course, a caring limited to one's biological children but one that extends to a wider community. Moreover, it supplants the emotional connections and mutual loyalty that may initially bind lovers or spouses but which, Tawfiq's stories strongly suggest, rarely if ever last.

Under the fierce gaze of social sanction, that connection may not even have a chance to germinate. "Jealousy, Love, Illness, Pain, Peace, Mercy"—the title itself suggests an emotion-ridden journey of personal connection—is a complexly narrated story that, unlike Tawfiq's others, is set in an Egyptian village. As the structure of conventional marriage is celebrated through familiar ritual, the longings of those who do not quite fit into this little world remain unacknowledged. The first narrator seems to be a village woman who is everywhere and nowhere, a fantasy figure akin to the supernatural characters of some folktales. But she also is a down-to-earth participant in the wedding festivities of the young, model couple, Amina and Rabi`. The elusive Muhammad—who is both "stranger" and "strange," insider and outsider, who has a mother in the village but chooses to live in his hut in the field—cannot locate, within the socio-linguistic conventions of his community, a language in which to realize his own dreams.

This story shares with "Points of the Compass" not only the imagery of motherhood but also a forceful reliance on the structures of oral narration. In addition to figures who seem drawn from the characters of Egyptian folktales, structural and linguistic features signal this strategy: repetition, the occasional echo of conventional phrases that address an interlocutor, and the assumption of a shared local frame of reference. In "Jealousy, Love, Illness, Pain, Peace, Mercy," Tawfiq uses the conventions of familiarity to defamiliarize. Circularity and repetition—always within a shifting context—together with the assumption that the reader knows who is speaking, all draw us into the storytelling community while simultaneously distancing us from it. Logocentric conventions overlay the structure of personal narrative, of oral storytelling: the formalized structure of separate and progressive sections (preamble; exposition; passage, i.e., "paragraph" or *faqra*); the suggestion of factual statement, which is then undermined by the effect of the oral; the injection of "rumor"; and the different voices. Thus, Sahar Tawfiq joins other Egyptian fiction writers and poets of the 1980s in probing Egypt's oral narrative heritage and suggesting its links to the folklore of other communities[4] while suggesting how appropriations of this heritage are themselves mediated through the written word.

• • •

Sahar Tawfiq's sense of histories and connections, of migrations and returns, appears most complexly in the ambitious "Points of the Compass." In addition to drawing on orally transmitted community expression, especially the folktale, she utilizes another resource that has captured the attention of fiction writers increasingly in recent years: ancient Egyptian cosmology as expressed in the art and literature of Pharaonic Egypt. One interesting feature of this story is her exploration, through the juxtaposition of motifs, of connections between ancient Egyptian beliefs and more recent community practices and narratives. What makes the story particularly compelling is that its structure—that of embedded and interlaced storytelling, of many voices telling both tales of the past and personal narratives which are no less a part of community lore—perfectly embodies the mytho-historical imagery that runs through it like the river that also gives it structure and direction. The result is a concept of Egyptian history that gives prominence to community memory and to the individual trajectories of those whose stories are not told in official histories; that speaks to the importance and interrelatedness of material and mythic geographies; that poses different times and places and processes as simultaneously existing; and, finally, that puts female figures and gendered experience at the center of an alternative history, one that does not separate or hierarchically order "fact" and "fancy."

The inclusiveness of this history is suggested in the geo-mythic perimeters that give the story its title. "Points of the Compass"— literally "the four directions" (and *jiha* denotes both "direction" and "side," thus both movement and placement)—echoes the four cardinal points of ancient Egyptian cosmology, which were often symbolized as the four pillars that held up the sky. But they also suggest the movements of the Nile, flowing from south to north, flooding to east and west, and giving life to the land of Egypt. It is with this movement that the story begins, with a description of the flood which, until the completion of the first Aswan Dam in 1902, soaked the land and brought a new layer of soil each year. This natural renewal meant a rich harvest, whereas in recent times, as a canal system has replaced the annual flood, exhaustion of the soil has been a major problem.

This river of renewal is "the sacred river." The first sentence of the story conveys both the life-and-death importance of the Nile— recall Herodotus's oft-quoted declaration that "Egypt is the gift of the River"—and the related centrality of a sacred river in ancient Egyptian belief systems. The river is both inside of human history and outside of time: in the story, no specific time reference orients us, although in its later sections it is clear that the present as well as the past are both part of this history. This in turn reminds us that it is not so much what the beliefs and practices once represented—let alone what they "really were"—that is significant to recapturing them now, but rather what imaginative and social uses they have been put to more recently. Sahar Tawfiq's Egypt of the Pharaohs is not that of an archaeologist but rather that of a twentieth-century village or city dweller, imbibing some layers of the past in school, learning some from elderly family members, and taking in still more with the proverbs and religious invocations that are part of everyday speech.

For example, the survival of a sense of "the four corners of the earth" in popular belief is suggested by oral narratives that have combined an Islamic framework with the notion of the four pillars. In some tales, the four major *awliya* ("friends of God," loosely translatable as "saints" in this context, known as the *aqtab* [s. *qutb*]) are said to each have "his own post and his own job. They carry the earth, each from his own quarter."[5]

The four points of the compass were also where the limbs of the sky goddess, Nut, touched earth, and the four pillars could become her four limbs. Just as she arches over the world—over Egypt—and over the tomb or the sarcophagus in protection, Nut's body also canopies this story. At the end, her image rises with clarity as *Amm* `Ali's "one and only love" tells him that she "grew and stretched like a blossom of light." But throughout, Nut is present in her many facets. Nut is the sky goddess, granddaughter of the sun god, and was born of the union of Shu, the air, and Tefnut, moisture. Wife to her brother, Geb, the earth god, she bore the famous quartet: Isis, Osiris, Seth, and Nepthys. Geb, the earth, lies flat beneath her as she arches over, her feet planted in the east and her head and arms to the west, her hands on the periphery. Her whole body, encased in a long blue gown, is etched with stars. It was believed that she swallowed the sun god each night, protecting him as he sailed through her body and emerged between her legs each morning.

Nut had other roles in the Egyptian belief system. As the Old Kingdom Pyramid Texts show, when the reigning king died and was about to join the gods, it was Nut who would stoop to carry him up to the heavens.[6] Thus she had a protective role, inscribed in a maternal image, with respect to both the sun god and the kings, and then, later, with respect to the immediate afterlife of less exalted Egyptians.[7] This image echoes through the story—and also through "Jealousy, Love, Illness, Pain, Peace, Mercy"—as the mother who surrounds, envelops, takes in, and then gives birth, protects.[8]

The image of Nut therefore combines aspects of creation, maternal protection, the maintenance of cosmic order (as the being who separates the earth from forces of disorder), and also sustenance and fertility, for it is she who makes the sun available to growing things. In Tawfiq's story, a mother's children are likened to growing plants (also symbolic of life to the ancient Egyptians) who flourish in the sun, specifically the Egyptian sun. Thus Nut is linked to light ("I grew and stretched like a blossom of light") and to greenness of both plants and the stars. An ancient royal prayer to her says:

O great strider
Who sows greenstone, malachite, turquoise—stars!
As you are green so may Teti [the king] be green,
Green as a living reed![9]

In Tawfiq's story, Nut—or rather the earthly woman who journeys and transforms herself into a Nut figure—seeks to create in a different way. Rather than sowing stars, she inscribes letters that metamorphose into human images: "When I wanted to write—with the color green—the letters of the heavens and the earth, I dipped my pen in the new plants and drew the face of a person." Writing, acts of creation, the fertility of the earth, acts of motherhood, and storytelling—for this is narrated to the old man, *Amm* Ali—are all linked.

But the end of the story—or its temporary end, for *Amm* Ali may well have more tales—also evokes the trajectory of the earthly king as he becomes a god, for the female figure, like the king, "frees [her]self from the fetters of the earth," from an earthly paradise of date palms, reminiscent of the paradise described in the Qur'an. The final movement upward echoes the climax of the Pyramid Text in which the royal supplicant "prays for admittance to the sky."[10]

But this spiritual flight does not dissipate earthly realities. In today's world, Egyptians in search of a livelihood move outward to all points of the compass, as another narrator, Mufida, describes in anguish. Her husband left; her sons leave. Emigration touches most Egyptian families. She tried to go, too, but "the sun there is not our sun, nor are the plants and trees ours. . . . it was all so strange that I had to come back." Her son questions whether he is Egyptian. Does this notion of identity, of belonging and community, have any meaning left?

Tawfiq explores this question of belonging, of history, not only through her evocation of Pharaonic cosmology but also through the lens of folklore—community beliefs as organized and expressed in practices of storytelling and ritual celebration. Then she links these to the ancient images she has constructed. The figure at the end who "writes with the color green" is inscribing faces that bear the contours of all of this history.

In the first section of the story, "Westward"—the first direction, that of the sun's path and of the flood—Tawfiq's rewriting of an ancient ritual, that of the Bride of the Nile, organizes this history. Each year just before flood time, the Egyptians were thought to have cast an effigy resembling a young virgin girl to the Nile to ensure that it would rise.[11] The practice survived in the form of an annual festival at the rising of the Nile in which a wooden doll dressed in bridal clothes was thrown into the river.[12]

There have been various correlates to this practice in oral narratives. In certain tales, a virgin (or "bride") is thrown to a crocodile or to a serpent who will keep the Nile waters back unless it receives this sacrifice.[13]

In Tawfiq's story, this practice is linked to a past in which the river brought fertility and to a present in which it does not. Structurally, it encompasses another tale, one that this narrator's mother tells her, of an old man who was supposed to give all Egyptians water from a magical waterskin. "At the time," says her mother, "Egyptians needed that sort of thing, but now nothing is of use to them but the water of the Nile." Yet this disavowal is countered by her mother's narratives.

As the girl, clad in a wedding dress that her mother has embroidered, goes to the Nile, she concludes her narrative to *Amm* Ali ("then" the young man by the mill, "now" the old man by the river who relates all of these embedded tales to an unnamed, collective narrator). She advises him to dream, whereupon he picks up the narration, relating the rest of the legend/event as a dream. The bride, surrounded by the singing crowds of festival time, "drew near to her bridegroom and raised her blood-red-hennaed hands." But this "sacrificial victim"—who, unlike those of old, chose this route—does not disappear into the water. Instead, *Amm* Ali (as his younger self, the young suitor) sees her "sitting in the eye of the sun, a crowned queen." Now she is the Lady of Heliopolis, the Eye of Re; she is Nut, "queen" rather than "victim." This is juxtaposed with the image of the stalks of wheat that are made into good-luck ornaments[14] at harvest time. These may be further associated with the Coptic custom of making Palm Sunday fronds into good-luck charms. In this cluster of images, Tawfiq beautifully brings together Nut and the Bride of the Nile, the whole cycle of growth and renewal (from flood time to harvest time), and Coptic, Muslim, and ancient Egyptian practices, all in a female figure who makes her own choices, narrates her own story,[15] and is transformed from sacrifice into goddess.

As is already evident, "Points of the Compass" is constructed as a series of overlapping and embedded narratives, thus incorporating a sense of oral storytelling—mother to daughter, lover to lover, old man to young listeners. There is no "frame story" beyond *Amm* Ali's serial unfolding of experience, which itself consists of stories he has been told. In a sense, the point is simply to keep telling tales, to keep them alive, and to reaffirm the importance of the dream and the myth in constructing one's own history. But on another level, the point is to retell a community history in which "myth" and "material life" have no separating boundary. This is reiterated—if also made more confusing—by the impossibility of totally separating the narrative voices that tell the story. It is also emphasized by the difficulty in ascertaining the exact relationship among the women whose stories are retold by *Amm* Ali (a reincarnation of the wise old man of folk narratives, who points the way and offers wisdom on the river bank),[16] or the relationship between *Amm* Ali and "Mufida's poet," or the relationship between the wise old man and his interlocutors. It is not made clear who gets the last word in this tale. The dream as a journey (*Amm* Ali says, "And thus I slept . . . and journeyed."), history as a journey of many voices, history as a dream, creation and fertility as wonders that we must somehow encapsulate in images— the poetry of Sahar Tawfiq's story offers a modern cosmology that dislocates those on which it is built.

• • •

Working in the late 1980s on an anthology of short stories by eight Egyptian women writers, I happened upon Sahar Tawfiq's own collection of short stories and was excited by her sparse yet poly-phonic diction, her often abstract yet metaphorically rich imagery. I knew immediately that I wanted to include some of her tales in my anthology. Living in Cairo at the time, I set off to find her, which proved to be the sort of circuitous journey that some of her own stories describe. She had no phone then; none of my literary acquaintances knew where to find her or whether, indeed, she was anywhere in the vicinity of Cairo. Was Sahar Tawfiq just a disem-bodied collection of printed tales?

Finally I got hold of an address, the only familiar element of which was the area "al-Haram," just north of the Pyramids ("al-Ahram"). I set out. A helpful taxi driver tried persistently to find the right side street off the main thoroughfare leading to the Pyramids. We swung round five or six times, covering the same stretch of main road, and finally found an ill-paved side street that dived steeply downward behind a pharmacy, off the built-up expanse of the thronged main street. Relieved, I got out, thanking the equally relieved driver profusely for his trouble. But it soon became evident that I might be no nearer my destination. The address wasn't on *this* street; a shopkeeper waved vaguely towards a broad, unpaved expanse, a sort of ill-defined, muddy square on and around which squatted buildings of various heights, some lived in, others unfinished. He didn't know, he said; he had never heard of this particular address, but perhaps it was down there. I wandered down, drawing stares both blank and curious. Knowing that *bawwabs* (who combine the jobs of building custodians and doormen) are usually rich sources of local information, I asked one, and he asked someone else. No one recognized Sahar's name; no one even looked at the address. Finally the home of Adel al-Sharqawi—the sculptor—was pointed out to me, for perhaps what I sought was *baytuh:* his house, but also by metaphorical extension, his wife. Feeling that I was living one of Sahar's stories of urban wandering, I headed for the little, almost rural house crouched amidst the multistory buildings and announced by bits of plaster sculpture leaning against its facade.

This little house encapsulates much that is characteristic of life today in Cairo. As you approach the turnoff from the main boule-

vard, the Pyramids loom just ahead, visible even above the apartment buildings, for Sahar Tawfiq lives in one of the neighborhoods
that have sprung up over the past couple of decades, across the agri-
cultural land that stretches south, as Cairo has overflowed its urban
boundaries. The small house was surrounded by fields when Tawfiq
and her husband moved there. Now engulfed, it seems an appropriate image of the kind of still point for which Sahar Tawfiq's characters seem to yearn, but which is endlessly hard to locate and to
maintain unencroached. Today's pressures do not stop at the door:
the landlord wants to demolish this house to construct a more lucra-
tive apartment building.

A native of Cairo and a schoolteacher, Tawfiq (born in 1951) first
published one of her stories in 1972. In 1985, her collection *An
tanhadira al-shams (That the Sun May Sink)* came out in Cairo. She
has also published stories in several literary journals in Egypt and
elsewhere in the Arab world.

Tawfiq has recently performed her own migration, one many
Egyptians have made. In 1991, she took up a teaching position in
a village near the city of Madina, in Saudi Arabia. There, she began
to explore local history. After a hiatus and just before her return to
Cairo in the summer of 1994, she began to write again and is cur-
rently working on a novel as well as composing short stories. The
present collection spans Tawfiq's writing career and includes stories
not in her published collection. "Doll" was written in 1975. "The
Time That Is Not This" was composed in September 1993 in the
Saudi village of al-Suwayrqiyya and was translated for the present
volume before its first published appearance in Arabic, in the Cairo
weekly *Akhbar al-adab (Literary News)* in September 1994.

As this introduction has attempted to show, many voices run
through the stories of Sahar Tawfiq. They are not always distin-
guishable. They converge; they echo each other across stories. There
are repetitions of language, too, within and across these stories/
poems, which I have tried to capture in this translation without
acceding to a tedium that tends to mark repetition in English more
readily than it does in Arabic. Tawfiq's strategy of repetition is
founded on an exploration of how words have multiple significations

that are simultaneously present but may carry different force at different moments in the text. I can only hope that the compromises a translator inevitably makes have been, in this context, successful.

NOTES

1.   Specific contextual information is given in notes, to be found at the end of "Points of the Compass" and some other stories.

2.   Published in *The Smell of It: Short Stories of Egypt and Cairo,* trans. Denys Johnson-Davies (London, 1971). The full Arabic text was not published until 1986.

3.   See also Sahar Tawfiq, "In Search of a Maze," in Marilyn Booth, ed. and trans., *Stories by Egyptian Women: My Grandmother's Cactus* (Austin, 1993).

4.   Tawfiq says she has consciously drawn on Greek, Roman, Chinese, Indian, and African, as well as Egyptian sources in her writing.

5.   This is from the translation of a tale narrated by A. Mahmoud in 1970 to folklorist Hasan El-Shamy. See Hasan El-Shamy, *Folktales of Egypt* (Chicago, 1980), p. 150. See also pp. 141, 149, 277 for discussions of this motif.

6.   See Miriam Lichtheim, *Ancient Egyptian Literature,* vol. 1, *The Old and Middle Kingdoms* (Berkeley, 1973), p. 34.

7.   See George Hart, *A Dictionary of Egyptian Gods and Goddesses* (London, 1986), pp. 145–46. For images of Nut as mother, see Lichtheim, *Ancient Egyptian Literature,* pp. 41, 44, 46. She says: "When entrance into the sky had become the central goal of the royal funerary cult, the sky-goddess Nut, mother of the gods, became the protecting mother of the dead."

8.   See Hart, *A Dictionary,* p. 145: ". . . it is clear that the underlying concept of Nut is that of the 'great who gives birth to the gods.'"

9.   Lichtheim, *Ancient Egyptian Literature,* p. 41.

10.   Lichtheim, *Ancient Egyptian Literature,* pp. 49–50.

11.   According to some accounts, the ancients actually sacrificed a living woman, but Egyptologists today believe this unlikely. According to Lane, the Muslim general who took Egypt in the name of Islam in 641 C.E. tried to halt the Bride of the Nile ritual. But, this legend has it, when the Egyptians were prevented from making their sacrifice, the river did not rise for three months, and not until a note from the *khalifa* (successor to Muhammad as head of the Muslim community) invoking divine power was thrown into it instead—a sort of compromise from the new, foreign rulers. On the Bride of the Nile ceremony in nineteenth-century Egypt (which had another component, a structure called a "bride" which was washed away as the floodwaters rose) and the story about the Muslim conquest, see Edward W. Lane, *Manners and Customs of the Modern Egyptians* (London, 1836, 1895), pp. 486–90.

12.   In Arabic, the same word, `arusa, can mean both "doll" and "bride."

13.   See El-Shamy, *Folktales,* pp. 8–9, 22, 159–60. Atum, the originary Egyptian god figure, is said to have first taken shape as a serpent, arising from

the primeval waters, Nun, which had some association with the Nile. Perhaps here is another link between ancient Egyptian practices and the serpent-river-sacrifice motif in these tales.

For another use of this motif, see Neamat el-Biheiry, "Your Face, My Children and the Olive Branches," in Booth, *Stories by Egyptian Women.*

14.   A further linguistic link echoes here: these ornaments are called `arusat al-qamh,* "the doll/bride of wheat," paralleling `arusat al-Nil,* "the Bride of the Nile." On this practice, see Winifred Blackman, *The Fellahîn of Upper Egypt* (London, 1927), pp. 171–73.

15.   That her story and all the others are then narrated by *Amm* Ali should be kept in mind.

16.   See El-Shamy, *Folktales,* p. 103, for an example. There is also an "old man" in "In Search of a Maze" and in "Jealousy, Love, Illness, Pain, Peace, Mercy." Unlike *Amm* Ali, they never speak.

VISITING THE OLD CITY

With a wave of her arm, she pointed out the ancient street and then started down the dusty slope. On every side she noticed the shops and houses that had gone up. She peered into all the shops. She saw the people sitting out front and inside and more people sitting at the coffee shops and moving along the street and gazing down from windows and balconies. She could see their eyes watching her or not watching her. She walked slowly from the dead-end alleyway out to the breadth of the street. She saw the stagnant pond filling the street. Plants had come up right in the middle of the street, rising through the stinking water. The house was still standing, still there. The small enclosed balcony and all the windows were shut tight. The little iron gate, now slightly open, had rusted over. She gazed at it, came to a standstill. She started off again, changing direction, heading toward the other alleyway. She strolled through the small streets.

That far-off day . . . I'd been coming here daily. I'd buy vegetables from the tiny shops. I'd shove open the rusty little iron gate. I'd go up

Sahar Tawfiq, "Ziyarat al-madina al-qadima," in *An tanhadira al-shams* (Cairo, 1985), pp. 45–49.

the stairs, into the apartment. I'd cook something and eat it. From the balcony I'd look up into the wide-open sky. To the grocer I'd say "good morning." To the butcher, the barber, the greengrocer, the neighbors, to everyone, I'd say "good morning." I'd lay my head on the pillow. I'd hear the children's shouts, the voices of people going by, the voices of neighborhood people staying put. I'd read the morning paper and other things. But when I went away, it was never to return. It wasn't important, then, that I come back another time. I don't know now if it was important or not. But what actually happened was that when I left, it was never to return.

That day the airplane was set to take off in an hour's time. . . .

I stare beyond the diminutive metal railing. Everywhere lots of people are moving to and fro, and I am not crying. I resume walking along the empty course as night fills earth and sky. The massive car moves quickly; I stare at the columns of light it leaves behind—columns of light and small trees moving backward. I stand still in the middle of the square, and I see the new columns giving off a yellowish light from their voluminous lamps. I see the people, commotion, cars, buses, the great hotel. I lose my memory of everything and ponder the things that appear anew. I buy a book, sit down in the coffee shop, and read. I drink coffee and wait for something, anything that might happen.

She returned from the alleyway to the main street. She looked at the house once again. She went up to it and gave the rusty iron gate a push. It screeched open. She mounted the stairs and eyed the door. She noticed the massive lock; lightly she knocked. She knocked again, knocked, knocked, knocked. She knocked hard with both hands. She went through her bag looking for the key. She searched for it in the corners of the building, between each step, behind the iron gate, everywhere.

I used to put the key in the inner pocket of the bag, but it's no longer there. And there's no one inside to open the door for me. From the day I went away, I haven't known where I put the key. Perhaps I threw it into the Nile one time, or maybe I tossed it out the bus window while the bus was moving, and I don't know who found it. But I think I put it on the table in the coffee shop on that very day and left it there. It was absolutely necessary that I put it on the table and leave it, for I didn't know whether I'd decide—or not decide—to return. To be honest, I'd forgotten about this, for I wasn't giving any thought to anything. But today I want to open the door and go in. I'll go on knocking; maybe someone will open it, but I expect no one will because there is no one there. And as for that burly man who is staring at me from the other door, I don't know who he is; I don't know what he wants from me. I wanted to keep him from grabbing my hand as I was starting to knock again, but I couldn't. I knocked with my other hand, and he seized it, too. I looked at him, not knowing what he wanted.

"Go away," he said.

"Good morning," I said.

But he said it again, "Go away!"

I told him that I used to say "good morning" to everyone. "And I'm saying 'good morning' to you, and this is my home, but what happened is that ever since I went away, I haven't come back. I don't know who put this big lock on it. I want to go in, but I don't have the key to it. No one has given me the key. I've looked for it everywhere, but I haven't found it. Could it have fallen into the swamp in which those dark green plants have grown? At that time, this big swamp didn't exist. There was just a little, boggy puddle, and the dark green plants hadn't taken root yet."

But the big man just said to me a third time, "Go away!"

"You can go ask the grocer," I told him, "and the butcher, the barber, the greengrocer, the neighbors, the children, the people going by. They will all tell you that I used to say 'good morning' to them. And not a single one of them said 'go away' to me. Now, will you just let go of my hand so I can knock on the door. Maybe someone will open it for me."

But the man said for the fourth time, "Go away."

She went down the stairs, out the rusted iron gate. She walked into the morass and with both hands searched in the putrid, standing water, snaking her fingers through the plants. She stood up, the water still dripping from her arms and feet and giving off a repugnant smell. She walked out of the fetid pond, looked at the grocer, the butcher, the greengrocer, the barber, the passersby, the children, and the neighbors.

"Good morning," she said to every one of them.

But to her, they all said, "Go away."

NOTHING BOUNDS
THE WIDE, WIDE ROAD

The blazing light of a hot
summer morning fell on my
eyes, and I woke up. Alone in
the bed, I remembered immediately that today might possibly
be the last moment in all the decades of this world.

I got out of bed. I stood up. I decided I still loved you. But you'd
begun to withdraw from me, and I had to resolve things, somehow.
The whole world in front of the window was empty, empty, and all
the windows, open or closed. People were walking along in the
street, and no one recognized my failure.

There was a time I used to say no. At that time (so very remote
it was), I hadn't yet come to love you. It was you alone who made me
love you. I went into the bathroom and washed. I looked for some
food in the kitchen but found nothing that appealed to me. I considered drinking some milk, but the thought of its fattiness in the heat
turned my stomach. I went into the other bedroom and looked at my
father and mother. Eyes closed, they were asleep. "Huh, their sleep's
so sacred!"[1] I muttered to myself.

Sahar Tawfiq, "Al-Tariq muttasi` wa-la shay' yahudduh," in *An tanhadira
al-shams* (Cairo, 1985), pp. 67–76.

I went into the third bedroom. My brothers were sleeping. In those few moments—and for the first time ever—our house appeared to be a peaceful, happy home.

But just a couple of minutes later it had all come to an end. My sister came in and asked if I'd made tea.

"No," I told her.

"You're so lazy," she said. "You woke up before any of us, but you haven't done a thing."

I didn't answer. My brother, the one who is still a child, came in. He asked for a piaster, and I scolded him. My mother woke up, came in and sat down, and looked at me with regret. I paid no attention.

"I'm going out," I told her.

"Where?"

"I'll go over to Mona's."

She didn't respond. I got to my feet and went and threw on some clothes, any old thing. I looked in the mirror, realized I didn't feel like putting on makeup. I quickly ran a comb through my hair, raking it straight back, and picked up my bag. Expelling a breath with each word, I spoke to my mother.

"Give me some money."

She examined me head to toe. Since I didn't have even a millime,[2] I repeated my request. She gave me that withering look of hers. Finally I decided to hang on to my last bit of self-respect and go out as I was. I decided I must look for a job so that I could have a sense of freedom, feel like my own boss. The last thing I could imagine was remaining in this state, always in need of others.

I went to Mona's. We exchanged kisses. We kissed each other a lot, but this wasn't any indication of errant behavior, for our relationship was 100 percent proper. We were totally on the same wavelength.

"Have you had breakfast?" she asked me.

"Yes."

"What's the matter?"

"Nothing," I said.

"Shall I plan to meet you today?"

"Yes," I told her, and then I added that she should come with me to meet you because she wanted to see you, and maybe you wished that, too.

She put on her clothes and stood before the mirror.

"Why didn't you put any makeup on?" she asked me.

"I don't want to. I don't have any desire at all to wear makeup."

"No, wait, put it on," she said, "and comb your hair in a way that looks better." She seated me in front of the mirror.

A while later we went out and walked shoulder to shoulder down the street. She asked me about our relationship, and I told her that I love you as I've never in my life loved anyone. I said that whatever sort of relationship I'd had in the past now seemed as if it hadn't happened to me but maybe to someone else, and I'd simply gotten to know the details somehow. I said I really believed so, in my own mind. And if I were keeping it from you—saying some of it didn't actually happen to me—well, I wouldn't be a liar because it's all the truth as far as my own inner conviction goes. Anyway, the only reason I tell you these things, I said, is out of some sense of real, bodily loyalty, pure and simple, and because what happened was just a physical thing, maybe. Now, though—and I believe it really didn't happen, or at least it no longer had any mental or psychological hold over me at all. . , . Well, maybe it *had* happened, but the whole business had been completely erased from my psyche by now. I could remember only isolated incidents, totally unconnected to my own emotional state.

Then I told her that when it came to you, I thought I'd been able (to a great extent, and at one point in time) to attract you to me completely. But yesterday as you talked to me, I felt as if we were strangers and that everything, if it weren't to end today, had ended yesterday. I felt that today all the world's sorrows were coming to rest on me; I hoped that you would once again smile at me without showing any bitterness. I told her that you were the stronger party, the continuation of our relationship was in your hands, and if you were to leave me, I hoped that it wouldn't be out of some sense of pity for the way I wait for you—because after all, to end that waiting of mine would be the worst punishment of all.

Mona was silent. She had no response to these things I'd said. A heavy ennui was bearing down on her, just like the dullness that filled me. We walked along side by side, me resting my head against hers, half closing my eyes. In all the people I saw, I was seeing only you.

We stood waiting for the Metro. It came, solid with people, so we didn't get on. We waited for the next one, but it didn't come. The train coming from the opposite direction arrived; it was crowded, too. A man was trying to get on. He was in a great hurry; he was running, but the train had already started to move. He leapt at a door forced open by the bulge of people, but apparently his foot slipped because there was nowhere he could put it. He fell under the Metro. The women who saw it screamed. The Metro went on, leaving the man behind, sliced in half, his blood filling the ground, a few bits of flesh scattered around the track. The men picked him up quickly, got him off the track, and covered his body with newspapers.[3]

We got off at Bab al-Luq. We pondered where to go. I told her I didn't have any money that would allow us to sit somewhere. Mona said she had fifteen piasters, and we could have a cold drink for about that much.

We sat down in one of the coffee shops. We were two hours early for our appointment there. I discovered that I was hungry and realized I hadn't had breakfast. I said as much to her, and she said she was hungry, too, and that we must have some coffee and eat something. But money was the problem, and we just couldn't eat without drinking coffee. But we couldn't have coffee on an empty stomach, either. Finally we decided to eat and have coffee, too, and if you were to show up, maybe that would solve the problem. But maybe you wouldn't have any money either, and the problem would still be there. We were kidding around mechanically, laughing nervously when nothing called for laughter. I told her that a woman had taken ninety sleeping pills to end her life, but then it hadn't ended, and that the Day of Resurrection hadn't yet been fixed on the calendar. Perhaps it would be today. I had dreamed, I told her, of my own death. One of those people had shot me, a bullet to my chest, out of treachery and nothing more. You were with me. I felt this enormous grief. I thought you were in as much pain as I was, and how I wished I could bear all of your hurting for you.

Finally I consoled myself with the thought that I'd had a very strong yearning to know what would follow death, and that now I would know and the uncertainty would no longer bother me. How I wished I could die and then come to you as you sleep and tell you all that has happened to me and assure you that I still love you. I felt the pains in my chest subside gradually; I felt myself being borne into another world. But I could move my body, so I hadn't died yet, after all. I called out to you.

"Yes?" you answered.

"Let's go find whatever doctor we can," I said to you, "so you won't die." I'll pull through because of my will to live and my longing to be relieved of my doubt—whether I go now or whether I stay on, to die later. But I don't want you to die, so I take your hand, and we stand up.

The man who had killed us laughed nervously, though.

"I didn't kill you," he said. "It was all a joke, and you didn't die."

And so I discovered that now there was no pain in my body, and you, too, were safe and sound.

Mona declared that this dream wasn't just meaningless babble, for I'd been feeling very tired, she said, and thinking bad thoughts about the future.

Curses on the future, I say; I don't want it. I used to have very great hopes, a lot of them, but now I see them to be nothing, just like the dream. I hope today will go on and on, and that you will stay at my side.

The food came. We ate slowly, in complete silence. I had no sensation of tasting anything, but I would eat since I hadn't had breakfast. The place was stiflingly hot. I slumped down, feeling completely limp, as I ate without caring what or how. With my hand halfway up to my mouth, I suddenly felt a complete lack of desire and stopped. I took a sip of coffee. It was terrible, but I went on drinking it. Mona offered me a cigarette, which I took. I don't smoke cigarettes, I don't like them, but I felt too lazy and sluggish to say no. I held the smoke in my mouth; sometimes I blew it out through my nostrils. Every so often I filled my chest and head with it, feeling some kind of repose. Even though I'd been with you just the day before, I felt an overwhelming desire to see you, to call you the sweetest things, to caress your name and everything in you. Another hour and a half! if only you would come early so I could see you sooner!

Muhammad came. He greeted us and asked about you. I told him you were to be here at one o'clock. We invited him to drink something, on us. He let us know that the weather was very bad, very hot, to the point where a person couldn't bear the clothes on his body. Eyes half averted, he asked me whether I truly loved you. I gave him a sidelong look and told him I hadn't yet settled on the answer to that question. It seemed we were just amusing ourselves, and I thought it would all end soon. He said he thought so, too. He asked me if I'd read the fortune column today. Apparently Saturn had moved into Gemini's path. To judge by that, the war would definitely end within two years. And a woman had been aflame, he said. Her brother claimed that her husband had set her on fire, but folks testified to the contrary. Her brother kept to his story, though: it was her husband who had ignited her. After this we were all silent for some time. Resting my head against the wall, I watched the door and waited for you. But there was still an hour and ten minutes to go. Finally Muhammad glanced at his watch and said he must be going. We returned his gesture of farewell with our eyes. He turned his back on us and walked out.

"How about going somewhere, anywhere, and then coming back just in time for the appointment?" I asked Mona.

"Fine, let's go," she said.

We got up, slung our bags on our shoulders, and walked slowly outside. The waiter called us. I glanced back at him and told him we'd be back in a little while. We went out. The street stretched so wide it joined the sky, and there was nothing to bound or constrain it. I put my arm in hers, and we strolled among the passersby.

"Where shall we go?" she asked.

"Wherever our feet take us. How about visiting Madiha at work?"

"Fine with me."

We went to the building where Madiha works and climbed the

stairs. One of her office mates, the one who was sitting down, said she'd gone out. We left them, descended, and were once again in the street, no time having elapsed at all. At that moment I longed to be in a spacious bus that held no people, had no seats and no dirty floor, no driver or steering wheel—a sealed bus without doors or windows that would take me as quickly as could be out into the wide world, colliding against trees, propelling me in all directions, knocking me against the walls until I fell, seeing nothing in the darkness. It would go on rolling me from side to side until I lost consciousness and couldn't open my eyes or recall the world or my mundane life. I longed to be alone in a completely enclosed, isolated chamber, pacing back and forth, back and forth, my eyes staring into the darkness, seeing absolutely nothing, back and forth, back and forth, until my mind would cease to work at all.

I recognized, after twenty-one years in this world, that all I knew was that the Nile runs from south to north and the winds come from the north and that the boats put up their sails when they are coming from the south and relying on the current but if they are coming from the north, they unfurl their sails.

"What do you think of the world?" I asked Mona.

She gazed at nothing in particular and did not answer me. Then she sighed. Wanting badly to cry, I remembered that when I take you along everywhere, your face always confronts me unsmilingly. When I find you before me, I tell you all and complain to you. But time is slow; it doesn't pass.

"Shall we go back?" I asked Mona.

"Yes."

We returned to the coffee shop and sat in exactly the same spot as before. We both leaned against the wall, exchanging glances silently, patiently. Finally I let out a sigh of relief, my eyes on you as you approached.

As I looked straight at you, I realized I'd known you were coming and that you would go away, promising to return another time. And you'd go. And maybe, after that, you wouldn't come back.

NOTES

1. *"Huh, their sleep's so sacred!"*   This plays on an Egyptian proverb, *Nom al-zalim 'ibada,* "The tyrant's sleep is sanctified." The usage communicates the narrator's sarcastic and exasperated attitude toward her parents.

2. *millime*   One-tenth of a piaster or *qirsh,* mentioned by the narrator's brother a few lines earlier. The millime is the smallest unit of Egyptian money and often serves as a figure of minute monetary worth. But in 1972 when this story was written, a *qirsh* still had buying power. One could buy a small packet of chewing gum or biscuits for that amount or ride public transportation for two piasters.

3. *covered his body with newspapers*   Just a few years ago, the tram running south from downtown Cairo to the industrial and residential area of Helwan was often so packed that this sort of accident occurred—as the author witnessed on one occasion.

DOLL

I'd been put in that remote spot. Occasionally he would come over, or from afar he would glance my way, and momentarily a serene reassur-  ance would take possession of his features. As for the others, they were viewing the goods offered, not missing a one. They moved about and shifted position constantly, back and forth, standing and sitting down, and they conversed on all sorts of light subjects. Sometimes he moved around with them; sometimes he spoke with them. Sometimes he would stand still, smiling or laughing, or silent. Or he would jump about and dance, jump and dance around. After a time he came over.

"How are you?" he asked.

I told him I was fine.

"How many have you produced?" he asked.

I showed him the things I'd made.

"Good," he said. "Actually, you're not as energetic as you should be. You should have made the other things, too."

Sahar Tawfiq, "Dumya," *al-Thaqafa al-jadida,* no. 8 (May 1984): p. 15.

He left me and sat down at a distance. Now he was spending part of his time reading and some of it talking. He got up and began walking around and looking. He moved so very far away that I could no longer see him. I busied myself with what was in my hands and with looking around. In a very short while he came up to me, jumping, dancing.

"Look at what I'm holding," he said. He was grasping a doll. When he turned the key, it twirled around for a time and gave off an irritating sound. He bounded away. He began showing the others, turning the key, bobbing up and down, dancing. Finally he returned, out of breath. He turned it and put it down beside me.

"Before it stops," he said, "you will have wound it."

I regarded the doll. As it went on and on spinning, I felt a burning hatred for it. I resolved not to rewind it and just to pay attention to what was in my hands. The doll went on turning, but soon it began to slow down. It went slower and slower until it stopped. I left it as it was. From over there he was looking on, but I occupied myself with what was in my hands. He came over to me.

"The doll stopped, and you didn't wind it," he said.

"True."

"Why didn't you wind it?"

"I hate it, and I don't want it to spin."

"But it must. Wind it."

I took hold of the doll and turned the key. The doll began to spin. He went away. I decided that I truly did hate the doll, that I wouldn't wind it again, that when he came back and asked me, I would tell him frankly and straight out that I despised it.

But what happened was that when the doll did stop and he came and asked me, "Why didn't you wind it?" and I told him that I hated it, he said, "But make it spin anyway." I took the doll and made it spin, and he went away again. Finally I decided that I would have to destroy it. So I did.

After a time he came to me again.

"Why did the doll stop?" he asked.

"Because I broke it into pieces."

"Why did you break it?"

"I told you—I hate it, and I don't want it to spin."

"Why did you destroy it?" he asked, his anger showing. "The doll absolutely had to spin. Come over here!"

He took the key. He wound me. "Spin!" he said.

I spun around. He was very, very pleased. He picked me up and began to jump about and dance. He went up to every person there, turned my key, and showed them, all the while cavorting to and fro. I went on turning, turning, while he said to me, "Spin!" Finally he went back over to where I'd been and put me down.

"Go on spinning, don't stop," he said to me. He went off doing his little bobbing dance and disappeared into the crowd.

JEALOUSY, LOVE, ILLNESS, PAIN, PEACE, MERCY

PREAMBLE

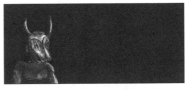

When I'm loving you, I want you to look at me and also look at the sky, the earth, people, all things, and to love all things. And then I surround and enfold you. I put you in my belly and give birth to you on the seventh day.

I pick you up and, bearing you, I fly far away, over the orchards, the cities, the deserts. I land and set you down in the blue, blue sea. I protect you from the eagles of the desert, the forests, the cities, and orchards. I build you a house out of reeds at the very edge of the woods. In it, and all for you, I put flowers, birds, books, music, colors, soil, the sky, the sea, the stars, trees, the moon and the sun, and all that you love and long for. I color its walls with the hues of the rainbow. From the stars' wings, I make a cushioned place for you to sleep.

And I call out to you, night and day. I prepare the fire so you will come to me, bringing the catch. When I kiss you, earth and sky tremble. All my ability and fortitude, my everlasting vitality, are gifts

Sahar Tawfiq, "Al-Ghayra. Al-Hubb. Al Marad. Al Alam. Al Salam. Al Rahma," in *An tanhadira al-shams* (Cairo, 1985), pp. 77–95.

from God. Through the night I dream of you as you sleep in peace. I let my hair go until it brushes the ground, and I cover you. I grant you peace and quiet; I offer you love and anger.

EXPOSITION: ON THE EVENTS SURROUNDING
THE MARRIAGE OF RABI' TO AMINA

In that remote place, there are no events. Only a few weddings, coming in their own time, within every seasonal cycle. Today it is the wedding of the slender, supple youth whom all the girls of the village hoped to have, and now those girls look on with the eye of envy at his beautiful, young, almost childlike bride. But the strange thing is that the stars in their sky were more numerous than the stars in ours.

I said to the old man that they were depriving us of the stars, that the stars in their sky were far more populous than the stars in ours, and that they were training enormous searchlights on the wider streets so we couldn't see the stars. Then they were filling those streets bordered by the huge lights with commotion and noise so we could not sleep or have any sense of peace and quiet.

Today is the *dukhla*, the ceremony of consummation. Yesterday the bride was paraded in all her finery. And the day before was the henna.[1]

On the day of henna, we went to the bride. We dyed her hands and feet with henna and tinged the hands of the children and the women's hands, ever painful from the constant use of water for laundering and cleaning. We lit the candles around the bride's feet and sang to her as we beat the drums. The next day we dressed the bride, ornamented her, and made her up. The bridegroom came and gave her the bridal gift. He sat with her for a short while and then returned to his own home. We went with the bridegroom and dyed his hands and feet.

On the last day, the bridegroom went to bring the bride to the house. They got in the taxi and circled the town; then they went to the house, where we welcomed them.

They set the basins down in front of the bride's feet so she could step into them, but she didn't put her feet in. Trying to avoid the basins, she stumbled. We sang and danced, and the men began shelling out money.[2] But what I don't understand is that after they'd done this, they said to us, "Go away!" yet they remained there, waiting.

A FIRST PASSAGE

The far-off house of dried mud stands beneath the vast sky saturated with stars: you mount and ride away. The stars shift position, ever circling around each other. I told you then to stay and to leave behind the many things. But you weren't concerned; you didn't consider any thing important. What was very important, though, was that you see the bride. It was important, too, that I understand why they demanded that we go away when they remained there, waiting.

Amina is a girl of fair tones. Her hair is like ingots of gold; her eyes are luminous stars. When she plaits her hair, the sun laughs to the earth. When Amina cries, the sky rains down a profusion of tears.[3] Amina was laughing and letting her hair fall loose the day she got married, and the whole world was laughing. The village girls were surveying Amina and saying that only Amina befitted Rabi` and only Rabi` befitted Amina.

I carry my child. I walk to the sun. When the thread of light meets my eyes, I rub my eyelids softly, teasingly.

From the heights, the whole world watches, and from the distant street, as I carry my child and step toward the sun. And I dream. When the thread of light meets the world, folks pace and stand still, sell and buy, and go to their workplaces, and I carry my child, and I walk toward the sun, and I dream.

I stand before the canal. I strip off my child's clothes, caress and play with him, set him down in the canal. The water immerses him, and the sun fondles his eyelids with the threads of light. My child laughs; I raise him to the sun. I put him down in the earth, and the soil clings to his little body. My child laughs.

By night I feel my way. I reach out my hands to grope for the great walls. I press the button that brings light. I watch you sleeping like an overgrown child. I sit before the heating stove, touching your hair, your face.

A SECOND PASSAGE

Furniture making is a profitable business—don't forget, you're not obliged to buy good-quality wood. Pressed wood, wood laminate—these are excellent, appropriate to the times, and they'll last. But perhaps it would have been better to keep in mind—when making your calculations—that furniture for the trousseau, for example, has to be handsome, even if, in any case, it's all a question of the price that's paid. But in the end you can always add a bit of charm through a few finishing touches that won't cost you much but will make it look like the whole business added up to quite a lot, really. If you're intending to go into this line of work, there are a number of things you have to take into account: the finishing, for instance, even if just on the outer surfaces, for this is very important, but time will have to be the deciding factor in the end. Believe it or not, I agreed to make this furniture six months ago, I swear to God; but what can I do, goddamn drugs and their pushers! Tomorrow the bride will be shown, and the furniture absolutely has to be ready so it can be put in the house. I don't know what's the importance of having so much furniture if the bride is going to her mother-in-law's house anyway. Complete suites for three whole rooms—where and how will they find room for all that? They built a new top story, especially for this, covering half the area of the house. Do you think the bride will prove worthy of the bridegroom's family? If the truth be said, she's a good girl, and besides, she's got a middle-school diploma. She's a good girl, one with some learning and polish, but between you and me, these women, this whole sex, there's no trusting them. You can't hazard a guess about what her morals will be, even right after she gives birth to her first child. She might turn into something altogether different, though this isn't for sure, either. Ah, my God . . . tomorrow is the showing of the bride. And what *is* for sure is that the furniture has to be ready, whatever happens. And my son is sick; I think he's got typhoid fever. His temperature went way up and then down two times in a row. Generally speaking, we can take care of typhoid, but he absolutely must go to the wedding; he loves these occasions. I think it'll be possible for him to go if he wears heavy clothes. Don't you think so? Goddamn drugs and their inventors! allow me, brother, to warn you against drugs. Be sure you don't give in to them. In fact, though, you might not be able to resist when you're sitting there in the coffee shop and you see the woman who runs it. . . . I don't understand how this woman can live like that, without a man, and have that kind of stamina. Definitely you can't sit in the coffee shop without inhaling some dope. One glance from that woman, and the boy crouches before you, sets up the pipe bowls in front of you—no, you can't resist. This boy you can't shake; how I hate him. The only one who couldn't care less is Muhammad. Only Muhammad can resist that woman, and the boy doesn't dare squat in front of him unless he himself requests it. I don't know how he does it. I think the only reason is that he couldn't care less, and in fact, he couldn't care less about anything. I'm going to make an important request of you: keep me from going to the coffee shop, tonight at least, because this work just has to get done. Help me, pal. Blend the putty—or, I tell you, I'll do that, and you do the rest. I'll help you with the sanding, too. You take care of the final coat, but hurry, work fast, don't worry too much about the quality of the finish. There's just no time, as you know; but you seem, in fact, to be quite skilled. I'll tell them I called out a polisher specially from the city; the most skilled *usturji* in town won't do as well as you've done. Where'd you learn this craft? I'll tell you something: why don't we go into business together? If we worked together, we'd make splendid things. But hurry, by God, I beg you! Tomorrow the bride will be shown, and, as you know, tomorrow can't go by before the furniture is all put in place out there in the house. But my son is sick, and he won't attend the wedding. You haven't told me, though, where you learned this trade. You seem to know many things, and in fact, maybe you know everything. God knows everything, too; will you agree to work with me? If you work with me, I promise you'll do well; but at that point, I'll have to really warn you off drugs, goddamn them all!

A THIRD PASSAGE

The tiny, far-off house made of dried mud is standing in the middle of the field that goes on and on: we gather firewood and light the fire. Tea made on a wood fire is the best tea in the world. Maybe the reason it's so good is the skill of the maker. Maybe then the reason was the heavy darkness.

I set my child down in the soil, and my child runs. He patters off over the ground. He clutches the threads of light. He jumps up onto the embankment and laughs. He takes hold of the sun with both hands and with it teases my eyelids.

By night I grope my way. I reach out to touch the great walls, so enormous, so high. *The old man looks at me. Long skinny fingers tremble as he distributes the slivers of dope along the clay bowls for the gooza. He puffs into the pipe and some water jets out on the ground. He sets the first bowl onto the pipe. He breaks up the coal on the filter into little pieces. He blows on the coals so that they glow and sparks fly. He puts the filter carefully over the bowl and begins to smoke. He tells me the story of the deviant who lured some of the schoolboys to his house and then attacked them.*

A FOURTH PASSAGE

Rabi` is absolutely the best of the village's youths. He's a man like no other: exemplary, upright, such good morals, calm, and easily abashed. Whenever he passes a woman in the street, he averts his gaze ... even if they do tell an odd story about him—a rumor, maybe.

The story, to put it simply, is that one time a woman came to visit his mother, a woman from the village, known for her sterling morals, her virtue. She was getting on in years, too. On that particular day, his mother wasn't in the house, and the strange thing is, as the rumor has it (and definitely it's no more than a rumor), Rabi` tried to force himself on this woman. Because she's a moral woman, very proper, she screamed for help, and—as was said at the time—Rabi` took fright, thinking about what might happen as a result of what he'd done, and he ran out of the house. When he didn't see anyone there, he hurried over to stand in his little shop that abuts on the house, as if nothing had happened.

But the truth is, this rumor seems odd indeed considering Rabi`'s good morals, and so it just can't be accurate, for Rabi` is mild, and he's easily abashed. Whenever he passes a woman in the street, he averts his gaze. And he loves his father and mother, respects his elder brother, respects all the men in the village who are older than he is. He never frowns at anyone; no, he's always smiling. He can be trusted, too. Buying or selling, he doesn't swindle folks. What sometimes appears to be cheating is just a mistake, unintended of course. He doesn't waste his time going to the coffee shop either; he doesn't smoke any substances. No, he prefers to stay in his shop until eight o'clock in the evening; then he closes it and goes home to sleep right away. He always speaks in a low voice, but he's got courage, and he's strong. You can see the steadfastness and patience in his face.

When Rabi` stands in his little shop, every passerby greets him. And then Rabi` finds exactly the right response. He asks about their health, and how are all the relatives? And everyone inquires about his health and the health of his sweet, good, aging mother. When Rabi` deals with folks, his bottom line is affection. He doesn't prevent them from getting whatever he has in stock: he doesn't hide anything away.

The really major problem came up, though, the day of the cigarette crisis. Rabi`'s allotment of good-quality smokes shrank, and that share had barely sufficed, anyway, for him and his brother and his close friend. At that time the other shopkeepers were selling cigarettes for more than the government-set price. But Rabi` was honest, and he wasn't willing to have a hand in such a thing. So he didn't sell to anyone. He went on selling the poor-quality brands of cigarettes, and kerosene and long needles for cleaning braziers. Yes, truthfully speaking, Rabi` was certainly the best of the village youths, and everyone loved him. Whenever he walked by at night, folks recognized his footfall, and they'd call out to him in greeting.

A FIFTH PASSAGE

The coffee-shop proprietor is a woman in her forties. She's a widow, tall and stout, and her face is round as the moon; her eyes are large and ringed by kohl. Her voice carries a force that silences men, and no one has any authority over her. Even her son—the young man with the thick mustache—even he can't say a word to her about leaving this sort of work to someone else, someone reliable. If the truth be known, nobody has any idea whether any man on his own is capable of mastering this woman.

The coffee-shop proprietor has a pair of emphatic eyes that level a gaze both strong and cutting. And when she swings those eyes around, the firmness of her back is evident to all. No woman in the village has a back like hers—ramrod straight and unyielding, rising elegantly from her buttocks. She has only to swivel around for every man in the place to suddenly shift his eyes to the ground, waiting. And if her voice rises as she stares down one of the men, there isn't a person in the village who can predict what might happen.

The coffee-shop proprietor has a pair of daughters who are like the sweet delicacy of the spring breeze. And they have a brother, a "real man," a fierce one, whom neither of them can possibly oppose. Even when he ordered them not to go to the bride on the day she was to be shown, they obeyed him mutely, still in a state of sleeplessness induced by the thought that they might encounter the two strange men who'd come into the coffee shop the day before. For it was then that the two strange men had made their way to the coffee shop. Their eyes had fallen on the girls' eyes, and the four had fallen in love. That night the girls had gotten no sleep or rest at all. All night they took turns describing their beaus to each other and plaintively voicing their worst fears. The upshot of it all was that each longed to marry her man, and how they wished their eyes could fall on them tomorrow at the showing of the bride! But when their brother—the fierce one—commanded them not to go, mutely they obeyed, and at once, and neither breathed a word. All they could do was sit in their room and weep.

The coffee-shop proprietor has a boy to serve the customers, a skinny youth with eyes that bulge out, you might say—a boy whose cunning shows through in the silence of his gaze. In his pocket he carries the dope and all the crucial equipment. He's quite skilled at the art of setting up the bowls and tending the *gooza*. The minute someone sits down, anywhere in the coffee shop, the boy goes right to his side. In fact, suddenly the customer finds him already there, seem-ingly without a moment's wait. With just a silent glance at his empty hands, he offers his services, tapping his pocket. He readies the *gooza* and has the first puff. All the men go to the coffee shop and smoke. None of the women smoke, though—that is, none but the old women who smoke hashish as they sit in the evenings, moon or no moon, at the entrances to their houses. Likewise, the two delicate girls, daughters of the coffee-shop proprietor, don't smoke, except at night after they've made sure their brother has gone out or fallen asleep, and after they've shut tight the door and window of their room.

All the men go silent in front of that stout woman, the coffee-shop proprietor, and they hang their heads and yearn for her, without letting on. But sometimes her son—the real man—will catch on. He can't say a thing, though. But what really jolted him was when she ordered her two daughters to go to Amina when she was to be shown, to deliver the money, the wedding gift, because she was too tired to go. Into the hand of the older daughter she put fifteen piasters, and she ordered them to go. But the son and brother (the real man, the fierce one) objected, saying he'd ordered them not to go. And when she just stared at him, he was furious. He hurried into his room, slamming the door behind him.

The coffee-shop proprietor's house has a garden in back that is full of pear and orange trees. In this garden appear a pair of girls as delicate as the buds just beginning to open on the trees. They scamper amongst the trees and pick fruit which they send with the gardener's little son to the two strangers sitting in the distant field. They perch atop the trees, stretching their hands up, up to the stars at night, letting down their hair in secret, concealing themselves from their brother. And they play, and hug the gardener's little boy, and each one longs to marry her beloved stranger, to marry her strange beloved.

A SIXTH PASSAGE

Muhammad is a strange man.[4] He left the village for the field. He built a house of mud brick with his own hands, a house of one room. He made four windows that overlook the four points of the compass and the land that stretches on and on. He made one door to the house, one door facing in one direction. In the house he put all the books and drawings he possessed and the single guitar. He promised himself not to go to the village except in dire necessity. He had only to dispatch one of the children to bring food from his mother's house in the village, to take the pots back and bring cigarettes.

Muhammad is a strange man. Everything about him is strange: his eyes are strange, singular; his crinkly hair, ringing his head; his dark brown beard. Undoubtedly a beard like Muhammad's would suit no face but his.

His hands are strange, the fingers long, rough, serene. They move unaffectedly, easily, looking relaxed. But on the guitar, they truly do look tense. Not just his fingers—Muhammad himself, all of him, is taut. His eyes glitter; his hair goes damp with sweat. When he is done playing, he sets his guitar aside and stares at the ground. He knots his hands in his lap and decrees a few moments of silence. If anyone speaks to him now, he will answer very, very quietly and tersely. It seems he doesn't like to talk at such times or have any words directed to him. Perhaps he doesn't want to have any conversation going on around him either, but at the same time, when he's in this state, he isn't capable of keeping others from talking or of getting worked up against anyone.

And the children, they would walk by Muhammad's house in the field, too, and sing out their greetings. They would sit before him as he played the guitar and question him about the strange sketches hung on the walls of the room. But they were too timid to ask about one particular drawing of a man and a woman. They didn't look openly at this drawing; they just stole glances at it when Muhammad was fully occupied with his playing or engrossed in reading or making tea.

The folks of the village would pass by Muhammad's house on the way to their fields and call out greetings. When his friends, the strange men, would come from the city, any of the villagers would show them the way to Muhammad's house, and then greet them each morning as they were on the way to the fields. And when one of his friends would come all the way from the city that is so far away, then Muhammad would make a rare exception and take his friend into the village. They would walk through its narrow, sinuous, grimy streets and go to sit in the coffee shop. Any one of the men sitting there would insist that Muhammad and his friend sit with him. The coffee-shop proprietor wouldn't interfere with Muhammad and his friend in any way, not even through the boy working there, because Muhammad was strange and respected. Besides, he'd shown no sign of desire for the woman who owns the coffee shop, and he didn't steal glances at her on the sly, for he didn't have (or seem to have) any problems in this area.

It happened frequently that Muhammad would leave the village and the field altogether, maybe to go to the city. Then he'd return without causing any controversy whatsoever. When people died, Muhammad didn't show up to mourn them, nor did he go to any weddings—except for just one, the wedding of Rabi`.

Muhammad, the strange man, and his friend, the strange man, went to Rabi`'s wedding. There they were hoping to see the two girls—delicate as the sweet spring breeze—the daughters of the coffee-shop proprietor. Neither Muhammad nor his friend dared address either of those girls directly or tell her what he wanted to tell her. They just longed to be able to marry those girls. But it seemed a most unlikely possibility, especially since neither man dared breathe a word of it to anyone—even when it came to pass that the girls were able to visit them one day in the room that sat in the field overlooking the four points of the compass, for Muhammad, the strange man, and his friend, the strange man, busied themselves the entire time fixing up a comfortable place for the girls to sit and making tea for them.

And the days passed, and no such opportunity presented itself again at all, until such time as Muhammad, the strange man, and his friend, the strange man, left the village and the field, never to return.

A SEVENTH (AND FINAL) PASSAGE

The walls are immense, and high, and pitch black in the night. The sky looks just like the walls and so do the people, the earth, and columns, and slabs of rock. In the night I feel my way; I feel your face and hands, and I embrace you. I uncover the face of the sleeping child; I take hold of the sun's threads and weave them into a big, big robe.

In the night I grope my way. Do you know something? In this little village, I used to sit down in the field, the land stretching forth around me. The land went all the way to the sky. As for their stars, they were more numerous than ours. I said to the old man, when we sat down together in a corner of the coffee shop (which had no ceiling or walls), "Do you know something? You have more stars than we do." While we were at the wedding, everything seemed to be lovely and just fine. We were singing and laughing. But the thing I don't understand is that afterwards they said to us, "You can go now, it's all over"; yet they just went on sitting there.

I feel your face and hands, and I embrace you. Bearing you, I make my way carefully among the people. I carry you to the sun, and I dream. I set you down in the water, and I dream. I strip off my clothes and sleep on the dusty ground, the earth clinging to my body. I watch the threads of light bearing my child; I watch them caressing my eyelids. I take the sun between my hands, and from it I weave a big, big robe. I kiss its threads one by one, and I dream.

NOTES

1. *Today is the* dukhla   This paragraph evokes rituals that mark a traditional wedding. The *dukhla* is the wedding night, supposed to be the night the marriage is consummated and the bride's virginity is ascertained. Traditionally, in a village wedding, the festivities may last three days, and the night before the *dukhla* is called *laylat al-jalwa,* "the night of exhibiting," referring to showing the bride in her full finery to those who have come to congratulate her. However, the *jalwa* and the *dukhla* may take place on the same day. The "night of henna" is the evening before the *jalwa,* when the bride's hands and feet are decorated with henna, inscribed in various patterns. Sometimes the groom is decorated this way, too. The next paragraphs describe further wedding rituals.

2. *began shelling out money*   This refers to the gifts of money given to the bride and groom by their guests at the *jalwa.* A member of the bride's or groom's family receives the gifts and records them so that the family will know to reciprocate appropriately.

3. *When Amina cries, the sky rains down a profusion of tears*   This echoes a motif found in folk narratives. For an example, see Hasan El-Shamy, *Folktales of Egypt* (Chicago, 1980), p. 65: "When the girl cried, it rained."

4. *Muhammad is a strange man*   The same word, *gharib,* signifies both "strange" as eccentric and "stranger." In this section, the author plays on the double possibility.

MOMENTS OF WALKING
IN DARKNESS AND SLEEP,
CONVERSATION AND WAKEFULNESS

We began our walk at one end
of that narrow, shadowy street,
the one bordered by a row of
scrubby trees and inhabited by
a scattering of dilapidated old

buildings. Unsmiling, he put his arm around my shoulder and held
it there. I leaned my head against his neck. Above us a tree worth the
name passed by and after it a scrubby one.

"Why not say something?" he asked.

"What shall I say?"

I really tried to say something, but I couldn't find anything to say.
At last something came out. "You know what? I like this street a lot."

"Why?"

*I like this street a whole lot, I thought. I've always loved it. We, too,
used to walk here. Our feet would lead us to this place, and we wouldn't
even realize what was happening. Every time we walked here, we
fought. He hated this street, this very same street. He used to accuse me
of deliberately coming to this particular street. But as for you, I know
you love it as I do, perhaps because I'm walking down it with you.*

Sahar Tawfiq, "Lahazat min al-sayr fi al-zalam wa'l-nawm, wa-l-hadith wa'l-
sahw," in *An tanhadira al-shams* (Cairo, 1985), pp. 51–57.

"Why?" he was still asking me.

"Just because—I like it a whole lot, and that's enough."

At that time, I told you I knew him, but perhaps I did not love him. Now, though, I know that I did love him, in spite of all the bad things and despite all the mistakes I made with him.

We walked to the end of the lane and turned onto another, a wide and quiet street. We navigated it, and also one that intersected with it, which was crammed with cars.

I used to stroll with him through all the streets, even the one we're walking down now. Even so, when walking with you, I've never caught myself thinking about him. But today he keeps coming to mind.

As we walked, he told me that in this world many things happen without our knowing. There are people dying, others being born. We don't know which moments of our own lives are the happiest or which are the most wretched.

I advised him that the whole world is worthless.

The whole world is worthless as long as we don't know the value of whatever we may encounter, not even the value of moments.

I pondered his telling me that he loved me more than anything in the world. That was at the beginning. Then he began treating me roughly, as if he couldn't stand me. So I put an end to our relationship.

I told him, too, that the worst possible thing in this world is the drive to possess. If it weren't for that, people would all be happy, I said. You wouldn't find one human being attacking another, fighting to get what the other had, and you wouldn't find that person fighting back to hold on to those possessions. Perhaps if that drive didn't exist, I said, this world would be free of war and political splits.

He taught me to feel jealous. One day when I went to meet him, I found him sitting with a woman he'd had a relationship with before he'd become involved with me. He introduced me to her and told her I was a relative of his. Finally she got to her feet, and so did he, to take her home. He left me sitting there. A while later he returned to me, laughing, and asked what was making me so silent, more silent than I should be.

"What would you like to have happen now?" he asked me.

I had my arm in his, and now I hugged his arm tightly to me. I told him that when I was with him I couldn't hope for anything more. I asked him whether he loved me. He replied that he couldn't be very precise or certain on this point. To be truthful, he said, there wasn't anything he could definitely pin down in this world. Sometimes you might think you were resolving something with the greatest determination and precision, but then, at a different time, you'd see another side of the same question, and you'd settle it on that basis. And then maybe, at still a different time, the very same issue would change into something altogether different.

That's really true, I thought, and I considered how I'd hoped that in my life—over the course of my whole life—I'd form a single love relationship, one that would last forever. But the only thing that seems forever the same is that I see things changing. And this changes everything.

"That's true," I said to him. "But how sad it makes me."

After that, I didn't want to talk. We walked a very long way. At last I told him I was tired and would like to go back. I would come to him tomorrow, I said.

I was sitting on the Metro, resting my head against the edge of the window, the wind hitting my face. And I imagined myself having to remain in this position forever; I imagined the Metro never coming to a stop. I looked at the other passengers, shifting about and talking, and in my mind they were transformed into the mechanized bodies of robots. As I went deeper into my imaginings, I couldn't fathom how these mechanical forms were able to move, nor could I visualize what was concealed invisibly inside those bodies, what it was that made them live and move and would suddenly vanish, leaving them inert. I couldn't believe, either, that all this would fade away, that it would all end up as nothing.

Everything was flickering by the window: houses, people, streets, shops.

At that time his face was passing by the window, and I saw his eyes looking at me. They swept me away, and I remembered all those things at once. I didn't dare tell myself that I really was hoping at that very moment to see him, and to complain to him, and to lean my tired head against him. I didn't dare admit that I was envisioning his chest as broader than this shuttered, narrow world. At that moment I decided that I must not come to you tomorrow and that I would bring it all to a close.

I longed, too, for an illness that would leave me in a daze, unaware of anything, and totally indifferent. Then I could behave as if it were my nature to be dull and unfeeling.

I stepped off the Metro and began walking through street after twisting street. I sensed that I was searching for something important that I had lost someplace. I wanted so badly just to go on crying and walking. I wanted the rain to keep falling overhead until I found it—whatever it was I had lost. But finally I gave up hope, turned homeward, and slept.

I dreamed that night that I was waiting for you someplace and that instead of you, I saw him coming towards me. He sat down facing me and looked gravely into my face. I asked him to get up and leave me because I was waiting for you. He said he knew and that he was coming from you. At that moment the coffee-shop walls looked to me like they were made entirely of glass, and the streets all appeared to be completely empty of people. I got up to search for you anyway. I went on looking for you everywhere, and I was crying.

The next day I woke up, put on my clothes, and went to him. He opened the door for me and welcomed me in. I entered the room, not saying a word. I walked over to sit down. He came and sat beside me, drew me to his chest, and began kissing me. He assured me that he loved me. I was looking around at all the things in the room and at his head in profile as it lay on my shoulder.

After a few moments he spoke. "Why aren't you saying anything?"

"What shall I say?"

"Do you love me?" he asked.

"Yes."

"Like anything?"

"Like something that can't be found in this whole entire world."

I began to stare out of the window, taking in the vast emptiness, as I pressed my fingers into his hair and thought about my dream of the night before.

Eventually he spoke again. "What I said yesterday, did it upse you?"

"No," I said.

And at that precise moment, I felt as if all things were losing their value—even me.

POINTS OF THE COMPASS

The river has four directions:
From the south it comes, and
    to the north it goes,
And over the eastern and
    western lands it floods.

WESTWARD

The sacred river comes forth from deep inside the earth, carrying with it fertility and growth. Its waters rise to inundate the valley completely, washing the black soil. Then the river returns to its banks, taking with it each year's impurities, which it will cast into the great sea.

The earth prays humbly and laughs, for it has been cleansed and blessed.

And we want to cross to the other bank.

We embark and set sail. We plunge forward onto the long path that stretches between the stalks of sugar cane and maize, going on

Sahar Tawfiq, "Al-Jihat al-arba`," in *An tanhadira al-shams* (Cairo, 1985), pp. 3–44.

until we have reached the western heights. Before we begin our climb, we rest under *Amm*[1] Ali's date palms.

Amm Ali's long black frame casts a shadow over our heads. We lie down, spreading ourselves across his patch of ground, and we wrap ourselves in his tales.

Amm Ali said: Long ago my one and only love left me. I used to meet her by the old mill on dark nights. I told her about love. I kissed her, she kissed me, and together we told our own beautiful tales. From our dreams we wove a light to illumine our return through the darkness and the still silence. But one day at dawn my love left me. I met her at daybreak knowing that she was about to go away. And it was then that my one and only love told me the story in its entirety.

My only love said: I'll tell you exactly what is going on. At night I fall asleep, and I dream prodigiously. I get up in the morning remembering all that I have dreamed, or some of it, or sometimes I remember none of it. I rack my brains until I can remember. And then the story suddenly comes full blown into my head. And when it does, I know what has already happened and what is happening now, and maybe sometimes what will happen. From this I begin; I let go of all that constrains me. I talk with people and I act—doing whatever comes to mind—because now I know.

From this I knew it would happen.

Really and truly—all the circumstances were pointing to it, and the slender, dark-skinned girl had told me something resembling it, and all events were moving in the same direction. But, in fact, I dreamed it.

I dreamed suddenly, in the middle of the night as I slept, entirely alone. I dreamed that we were walking down the road. It was very crowded, and we were running and shouting and pushing our way forward toward the bridge. Voices were coming from many radios that people had with them and from radios in cars and buses. The voices were shouting that everyone must go to the bridge.

And, indeed, everything was storming toward the bridge.

And . . .

Do you remember the tale of the silkworm? All the silkworms were clambering over each other wanting to reach the top of the pile to find out what was there. But, in fact, nothing was there—except that whichever worm reached the top of the heap of worms and rocks would topple down the other side.

And that is what there was. The other end of the bridge was falling into the water, and there was no chance either to go back or to tell the others. So I hesitated for a moment and glanced around. A voice that sounded familiar was shouting: "Throw yourself in! It is the Nile; it is really the Nile!"

When I awoke, the light was coming in weak and pale through the tiny gaps in the closed window. But I looked around and remembered all that had happened, and I knew everything. It had been ordained, and there was nothing further that I could do.

In the morning I told my father, "The curse will come down upon us." He gave me a long look and did not reply. My mother informed me (and she knows these things) that, had I seen a black cat during the night, it would have been bearing an evil spirit.

"Yes," I said to her. "But I didn't see one."

Finally my father spoke. "My daughter, it's no longer what it was in the past. For some time now, the watercourse has been blocked up, and that's the long and short of it."

When I went to the river that morning, I climbed down from the high bank and lowered my legs into the water. Soon I heard the river whispering to me, telling me a momentous secret. "Go, dye yourself with henna," said the river, "for tomorrow you will be married."[2]

I cried hard and returned home. I dyed my hands and feet and said nothing to anyone. But my mother came over and studied me.

"My dear, don't go."

With my head bowed and my eyes fixed on my feet, I replied, "But the earth is no longer generous with its riches."

"It is still the earth, though," she answered me. "Don't be afraid, my daughter. When we were young, very young, an old man came to our village one morning. He stood at the head of the road that leads from the fields into town and then branches off into the little side streets. He was holding a waterskin. There he stood, giving people water to drink from this waterskin that never grew empty. He went on giving water to every passerby, whether it was someone

entering the village or leaving it. Then all the folk from the vil.
came crowding around. Staring at him and at his waterskin, the
began to drink. They were watching that waterskin very closely, but
the water in it never gave out. The women began bringing all their
children, even those still nursing, to have them drink from the water
of this blessed vessel. Only when it was growing dark did people
begin to disperse. Every one of the village men invited the stranger
to stay the night, but he refused them all and went away into the darkness—for all Egyptians, he said, must drink from this waterskin
before his death a year and a half hence, and he did not have enough
time left to him.[3]

"Did all the Egyptians drink from it?" I asked her.

Her mind wandered off for a moment. "I think so," she said,
"because he knew what he had with him and how much time he
had. He had enough. And he had enough stubbornness in his eyes
to repel all the specters of death for as long as it would take to carry
out his task." She gave me a long look. Finally she spoke again. "I
drank from it."

"Did my father drink from it, too?" I asked.

"Yes," she said. "I was a small child, and your father was a
teenager. Your father tells me that he drank from it, and that he saw
me, my mother holding me by the hand as she brought me to drink
from it. He remembers me, but I don't recall him from that time. I
remember only that old man with his white beard, his eyes encircled
by no end of wrinkles, and I remember the waterskin from which he
poured water into an earthenware pitcher. I remember seeing many
people crowded right around him and others standing at a distance,
all looking at him."

"All well and good," I said, "but I didn't drink."

"What does it matter?" she said. "At the time, Egyptians needed
that sort of thing, but now nothing is of use to them but the water of
the Nile."

"Yes," I said. "But it has gotten so low. It no longer floods its
banks."

I sat down on the ground, my legs stretched out in front of
me and my hands cupped around the henna. I told her what the

к-skinned youth had told me the evening before at the old mill.
also told her of the little things that had happened between us.

"I'll tell you, Mother, what's happening to me. I go to sleep at
night and have dreams. And then I know everything: what has
already happened and what is happening now, and sometimes, too,
what will happen in time. Yesterday I dreamed that the river was
summoning me. That's why, Mother, I am staining myself with
henna today. I want you to finish embroidering my wedding dress
this night and, Mother, on the bodice make a large sun.[4] Design it so
that when I'm wearing it, the rays will spread outward to touch every
part of my body. Embroider it, Mother, with all the laughing colors
there are."

My mother held me to her chest and began to sing me a lullaby.
She told me the story of the prince who crossed the seven seas[5] all
for the sake of his beloved, who was imprisoned in a tower that rose
seven stories into the sky and had no doors or windows except for a
single door guarded by seven jinn, giants. At the door leading into
each of the tower's seven stories stood seven other giants who were
even stronger and more fierce than the first ones.

Before hearing the story to its end, I fell asleep. Even so, I
dreamed of it during the night, for I knew that tale well. I saw the
prince as he slew the first seven giants, and I knew that he would
finish off all the others, too.

When the white thread of dawn clove the sky,[6] I sat up in bed
and discovered my mother still awake, embroidering my dress by the
light of a faint candle.

I eyed my mother. She laid the dress before me. "I have finished
it, my dear, but I have one thing to tell you. I drank from the blessed
waterskin, and you are going to the Nile so that all Egyptians may
drink."

"I know, Mother."

"You can avoid going."

"No, I will go."

She wept. "May God bless you, then."

I put on the dress and went outside. My father was waiting
for me.

"My dear," he said to me, "you can avoid going."

"But I will go, Father."

He wept and said, "Go then, and may God bless you."

And here I am, standing next to the old mill now, telling you everything that happened. Between me and the Nile lie twenty cubits, no more, and now I will go. Did I not tell you that I go to sleep and I dream, and that then I know everything?

I am going to the river now so that it will carry me to the western land. Then it will bring me back, in a new life.[7] Let it embrace me and feel sympathy for me and shelter me by its side, on its black strand. Every day I will dangle my feet in it. I will go right down to the water's edge; and then, when I descend into its depths, it will transform me into a tiny fish, swimming through its waters, so that it may kiss that little fish all over. Then it will take me back to the small hut where I sleep. Its smell will tickle me, and its pacific voice will sing me to sleep. A feeling of safety, of reassurance, will close my eyes gently, peacefully.

Here I am, standing before the river, a young and lovely bride going to it in true longing. Perhaps the river will come back to fertilize the earth as it once did.

And now I have one final thing to tell you: if you, too, want to know, then go to sleep and dream.

And *Amm* Ali said: Thus I went to sleep, and I dreamed. I saw those who lived on the riverbank emerging, all of them, silently before sunrise. They were exchanging glances, and it seemed as if they had an appointment to keep. The bride came out of her father's house wearing a black gown on which was embroidered a golden sun. Its threads gave light to the dawn, for they formed rays illuminated with all the colors of the spectrum.

The inhabitants of the riverbank walked behind the bride. They stopped at the door of every house and sang out to the children by name, and they called the men and women by the names of their children. They were singing a song. The children were coming out laughing as I stood alone at a distance, crying. Women were emerging from every doorway wearing pretty, bright-colored gowns and all their jewelry. When the procession started up again, the clanking of the jewelry sounded ever louder. Leaving all the houses on the riverbank behind, they made their way forward between the pale green hues of the sown fields. It was a procession of all colors, led by a gown embroidered with the golden sun. The trees swayed and bent down to ask; the singing and weeping answered them. At every tree they stopped and gave an account. The mournful whispering of the leaves responded. And then she drew near to her bridegroom and raised her blood-red-hennaed hands. The crowd turned around to go back.

When we turned back, we beheld the red rays stretching forth from the ends of the earth, crossing the sky over our heads. The rim of the great red disk edged into view as we made our way back, carrying our dried stalks of wheat.[8] When the disk came into full view, I saw her sitting in the eye of the sun, a crowned queen.[9]

SOUTHWARD

With the color green I wanted to write the letters of the earth and sky. But this was not enough. So I searched for the buried secret everywhere, in places both confined and limitless. But this was not enough.

So between the cramped and flattened lines, I told, one after another, the tales of children and of those growing old, of women and men, the stories of the sun and the hills, and of the only river that flows on steadily to the ends of the earth.[10]

I had to go to the ends of the earth to tell the story of the men who drew the sun and the gardens and the children of Adam. There the river had no dikes, and so it was wide and endless. It flowed ungrieving, touching the virgin banks to each side with the purest love and gentleness. The river was bearing the soil northward and strewing it over the hungry ground before flinging itself boldly into the great sea.

We crossed to the western side. There we sat under *Amm* Ali's date palms.

We lie down, spreading ourselves across his patch of ground, and we wrap ourselves in his tales.

Amm Ali said: And I have known many women. With wom‹
have journeyed to other lands. But I always came back, for afterwa‹
all I cared for was the soil.

Telling me stories one day, one of those women said: When I fell
in love with you on the very first day, I wanted to come with you to
the ends of the earth. I showed you the land that I love, and there we
built our house. We planted wheat at the river's edge; and whenever
the river flooded, we climbed the mountain, staying until the earth
was cleansed. The wheat would come up the next year, the stalks
long, bearing ears of grain the color of the summer sun.

In the morning you used to go out to the river, which ran right
by our house. You would stop at the embankment and watch the
horses and water buffalo go by on their way to bathe. You would
stare at them for a long time as they swam, the men hovering nearby
to wash and tease them.

As you were on your way back, carrying some of the green stalks
from the riverbank, your face would appear before me bearing the
traces of the sunrise, cheerful and expansive like the running water,
like the surface of the river that flowed right by our house . . . until
that day.

For the first time, you were late coming home. When I looked
at you, I saw that you had changed. When your eyes met mine, you
tried to tell me everything, but you could not. You thought I was
questioning you, but I did not ask. I left you, and I left that place. I
went to the coffee shop that you don't know about and sat in silence
watching the backgammon players. The long hours passed; I counted
them. When I came back, you were waiting. I never did know why.

That day you said to me, "I love you, and you alone. You are my
woman, and I have no other. I love you and know you better than you
know yourself. I know you when I am with you, and when I am not
with you. I love you, whatever I am doing. I love you when I am
walking, and working, and sleeping; and you are everything to me. I
know what is going through your mind, whether or not I can see you
at the time. I know what you are thinking about. I know what you
like, what you long for. I know you. And her? Well, she is like any
other woman; she has no part of me. I am not hers. I am yours alone."

He is not hers, he is mine alone, and he is not hers. He said so. He himself said that to me. I know him better than I do anything or anyone else, and he knows me. To him, she is like any other woman: she has no part of him because he is mine alone. He loves me, and he knows me.

That was what you said; it was all, but it was enough. I buried my anguish inside, and I remained silent, always. With each day the hours of your absence grew, and finally you were returning home very late every evening. I sat by myself. I watered and tended our few plants. I made your meals, and I questioned myself, only myself. I asked no one else, and I gave no answers. Finally I came to forget how words are spoken . . . until one particular evening.

In town there was a holiday celebration going on. At home there were lots of people, and they were dancing and laughing. You arrived late (as was your habit), but for the first time (and as was not your habit), you spoke gently and apologized. What I found even stranger was your gaiety. It was the first time I had seen you dance. Yet you danced as no one had danced before. The decorations looked strange, unfamiliar to me, and so did the lights and the people, and in the end, I could not fathom anything. It dawned on me that I did not understand. I would look at you, the sound of the drums making my head vibrate. Then I repelled the sound. I pushed it far away as hard as I could and fixed my eyes on you, but you did not look back at me. And then I knew.

I always understood exactly what the look in your eyes meant; so when you looked at her, I understood. Afterward I found that you were laying your eyes on her every day, and whenever she was away, you would go out to walk in the road, pretending to meet her by chance. You would wait for her at the embankment, and when she came along, you would be struck by surprise, as if you were seeing her for the first time.

That day you did not come home to me. Instead, you went off with her to wherever it was that the two of you felt like heading, as if you were lovers meeting for the very first time.

When I went out for the first time with the very first man I ever loved, we went to an enormous garden. We ran and ran. We threw ourselves down on the soft ground and rolled around. When the day was over, we were startled to find it gone. When we came to our senses, we remembered that we had forgotten to eat and smoke all day long. And now, every day, I imagine the two of you in the very same state, the same surroundings. There is one difference, though. Today I feel no happiness. Today is no longer like yesterday, for things have changed.

The huge structure was built on the hilltop, its head towering high in the sky, its roots sinking into the ground, its extremities spanning long stretches. Beneath its feet ships lie at rest, and the seas and land. Its extremities stretch on and on, and under its feet lie ships, the seas, the land, the rocks. Morning and evening, I can make out that edifice. Though I extend my hand to it, it does not see me. I climb up to it. It moves away from me. I embrace it, but it does not enclose me in its depths. I sit down right at its lowest layer of stones, and I am silent.

Look at her and let her look at you. Prolong your look, for what concern is it of mine? If you've already promised her, what does it matter? Or if you've sent word to her, or if you are waiting for her, or if she is waiting for you or on her way, or if many times you went away and did not return, what does it matter?

Each time your absence grew so long that I could no longer wait for you. So I, too, went away.

I boarded the ship. I put on my jewelry, prettied myself, and went down to the deck. I was on my own. Everyone else was with someone. And that man sitting with his companions was looking at me. I knew exactly how to talk to him. He knew, too.

As we conversed, everything was altered. Now I distinguished the sea, the sky, the ship. I took in the people, the warmth, the stillness. I saw him once in my life, one time which went on for days; I don't know how many. I know only that I did see him. He sat me down beside him and gave me a hug. He enveloped my shoulders and chest; he enveloped everything in me. He looked at me once, that's all. I looked at him, and I really did see him.

We sat on the ship's deck. Now we were together. With his own hands, he held the cup for me to drink. He hugged me, he fed me dates both sweet and bitter,[11] he enveloped me in warmth. And in the end the ship was docking.

We disembarked, and we were still together. We went there and sat down against the lowest layer of stones, and there dreams came true.

There is nothing else like it in the world. He smiles at me, I smile at him, and the two of us smile at everything else. But the sun was very bright, its rays casting light against secret walls that we had not been able to spot. When we did glimpse them and glance at each other and exchange our sad secrets—it was then that we hugged each other and cried.

Thus did things change.

And thus did I become close to another man and comfortable with his everyday ways, even though I knew that one day he would leave me before the sun had risen. And so I suffered greatly. But I knew also that if he went away, you would come back to me. Yet I no longer wanted you to come back, for he sits beside me in the emptiness, encircling me with warmth, and tells me a thousand tales.

The tales had not ended by the time he was to depart—for how could the tales end? But he went away. Before he left—never to return—we went together to the Great Pyramid. We sat at its feet and then lay down, gazing at the dark night sky, at the few stars moving slowly through it. I returned home alone, just as I had gone out alone. I put on all the lights but felt no warmth. I sat rummaging idly among my possessions and the things of yours that were still with me. I went to sleep surrounded by it all. In my sleep I saw my blanket flying away, and when I began searching for it, I could not find it. I went on looking, asking people in the distant streets and shops if they had seen my blanket. Finally I found it, but it was filthy and worn thin. I cried hard and did not know what to do with it. I was afraid of people's eyes upon it. I came back and hid it so that no one would see it. When I opened my eyes, the sun was halfway up in the sky and you were there. Finally you were coming to me. But today is no longer like yesterday, for things have changed.

No, today is no longer like yesterday. Things have changed.

The river no longer overflows its banks as it used to do all the time. The ground has waited, but the river no longer comes. In silence the ground has mulled over its grief, until year by year those sadnesses have piled up, and it no longer dares to laugh. No longer

do the blessed plants thrive. They have grown ill; their bough
weak and drooping.

Today is no longer like yesterday, for things have changed.

Finally you come to me. Finally you wait and come to me. But
today you are more distant to my gaze than the farthest reaches of
the great walls. Now I question you, but you offer no answer. Now I
know exactly what happened—that strange dream of return. When
I found the things I had lost, they were dirty and worn out. I hid
them in my wardrobe under the piles of clothes and sheets. And
today you come to me. What do I have that I can give you? I have
some food and a refuge if you like. Don't answer; just look at me.
Your books are thrown around everywhere. I don't know what to do
with them. And the dirty, worn-out things, I have buried them
beneath the wall.

NORTHWARD

In the dream I saw my love, his wings carrying him northward. I
called out to him, but he made no reply. I called out to him, but he
did not come. In the dream I saw the sky lit up with a thousand
colors, a thousand hues that extinguished the darkness. The trees in
that dream were growing and turning green; blossoms crowned the
treetops. But the other end of the bridge was falling into the water,
and all the people and cars, the women wrapped in black, and the
crowds kept on coming, coming from the other side.

We cast our lives into the embrace of the sacred river.

Amm Ali said: Every single one of them goes there with her.
There is no one who doesn't go, either by himself or with someone
else. And I'm just like them. I go as they go, I do as they do, but actually I don't know what they do. Nothing is as it appears, nothing.

Mufida,[12] the poet's woman, is a woman through and through.
Even her laugh, as expansive as Mufida is broad and tall, is a
woman's laugh. Her sharp and tender remarks, her strong stride, the
tongue between her lips, her clothes old and new, her grief, her
anger, everything in her—all her traits are those of a woman.

Mufida's poet is a man, violent and dissembling, rebellious and
deceitful, gentle and mysterious, valorous and cruel, gallant and a

rand, rascally and bold. All the qualities of Mufida's poet are tainly those of a man.

Amm Ali said: Mufida said: It was a long story, longer than it should have been. But let me tell you what I can. Perhaps I can speak truthfully, perhaps so. In fact, the only honest thing I can say is that I don't know.

The poet's woman I am; between my breasts he spends the night. But he only spends the night, and by God, what can I do?

Who is the naive one? You, if you're to believe me? Or me, if I'm able to make you believe me?

The children, yes, as I told you, they are all that is honest.

I was a little girl. My eyes comprehended nothing, my hair was a mess, and my father had died. My father had married two women; so I have many siblings, and they're all men. Only I am a woman. That's why my mother spoiled me. She used to hold me in her arms at night and gaze at me all through the day, combing my hair and dressing me up in a pretty dress. My chest began to grow early, and it quickly got large. Walking down the road, I drew the eyes of all the men, and then my brothers would beat me. My schoolmates joked with me and talked to me about sex. And as for that stranger—I had seen him at our neighbors' house. I don't know what made me marry him. Perhaps it was because my mother had died. Maybe, had I loved him, I would have gone with him to the ends of the earth. I didn't love him though. I only loved my children, who didn't love me as much as I loved them and who, after a brief spell, left me and went away.

"Come with me," my husband said as he was leaving to go to the ends of the earth.

"I don't know," I said then.

But I did go. There, the sky is strange, alien. So are the houses, the people, and the land. But I went. The sun there is not our sun, nor are the plants and trees ours. But I did go.

Objects and people stare at me, and I sense that I am far away. I work, I eat, I drink. I go out into the streets. The asphalt gives off no fragrance; the cars come and go indifferently. I go to work, leaving my children in the street. My children are little flowers. They are warm. They bear all the light. I leave them in the street, and I go to work. Objects and people stare at my children, and my children look at me. Their stares have lost the meanings they once had. They point to the sky, the ground, the houses, to all things.

But it was all so strange that I had to come back.

Here, under the sun, I set them down. I wrap them in my bosom, and I make them grow. They are warmed, and they grow in the soil, flourishing like home-grown plants. I smile and look at them, and I show them the green growing plants, the vast river, and the people. The warmth emanates from around them to rock me gently.

But they are not of me. They told me so and went away.

What a misfortune that I am of them, when they are not of me!

These are my own sufferings, so tell me, who is the naive one? No, don't say anything, for I have not yet finished telling how I married him—a man who does not know me and who leaves me night and day, returning only in the small hours of the night and then wanting to have sex with me. But I cannot.

I can't have sex with him when he is drunk. And I can't have sex if I'm angry or tense or when I feel no love for him, or if I know that he doesn't want me because I am me. There are women everywhere—and I don't want to have anything to do with him.

I have sex with him, understanding nothing.

He traveled on, though, and my children left me and went away, and so is the naive one me? Don't tell me, for I've finished now. Yet, I am not done.

Amm Ali said: Mufida's poet said: Mufida is not my woman, nor am I the man for her. She is not the woman for anyone else, either. She was that other man's woman, was . . . As for me, I am a poet, and never has earth or sky given birth to a poet like me. I have read everything and understood it all perfectly. Someday I will get married, but not to Mufida. I will marry another woman. I will marry a young virgin, yes, a young virgin, and when that happens, you will learn of it, and so will everyone else.

Amm Ali said: Mufida said: The poet's woman am I, but he does not desire me. I want him, but he feels no desire for me. I have tried all the methods; I've made amulets of all kinds for him; I've dressed up for him in the prettiest clothes; I have tried all the arts of women on him. But he does not desire me.

My brothers used to beat me, and my husband beat me, too. My children did not. Instead, they left me and went away. And he does not desire me.

I had three sons, three men. I loved them as no mother has ever loved her sons before. I held them to myself, and I brought them up. I gave them everything I had. For their sake I transformed myself into a man, and a woman, and a mother—into everything they wanted.

When the oldest one turned sixteen, he told me that I was not a mother.

"You're wearing yourself out for the sake of nothing," he said to me. "You are Egyptian, but I am not."

When he left, I shrieked until my entire body was shaking and the plates of my skull were trembling. No one heard my shrieking. And I had only two left.

But he came. And whom did he befriend? My second son. My first son had gone away, and it was my second son that he cultivated. And what a surprise it was that our house became his, and my son became his friend, and it was he who first introduced my son to women.

Together they went to all the places that my son had never seen. He got to know Egypt as he never had, and he went mad. My son went mad and did not understand: he went mad because he could not understand, and that was why he did not last.

In his company he comes home to me in the small hours of the night, either drunk or stoned, and always laughing. My son falls asleep, and he stays on, and we chat about everything. I tell him my complaints. At last we converse about love; but he talks to me as if talking, just talking and nothing else, is the best thing there ever was. When I told him I needed him, he answered me, saying, "You don't need anybody, no matter who that 'anybody' might be, or whatever the reason."

He did not realize; he could not understand, despite his being a man . . . until my second son went away. He was with me, and he did not realize.

My little one sleeps, and he sleeps, and I am alone. At night, in the darkness, I wake up, frightened by the sad dreams I've had. Nothing is visible around me. I get up and walk through the house,

from room to room, and I look at the door to the room where
sleeps, which used to be my son's. Several times I open the do
slowly and look at him, sleeping soundlessly. On the night when
got so frightened that I screamed, he came running, turned on the
light, eyed me, patted me on the shoulder, and went about com-
forting and reassuring me. I cried, and for the first time, he took me
to his chest and rubbed my back until I went to sleep, and then he
slept, too. In the morning I opened my eyes to find the little one
waking me up, staring at me, as he slept beside me. I got up and made
breakfast for the three of us. I looked at myself in the mirror and
found that my eyes were still red.

After that he slept beside me. We would talk and talk before
going to sleep, and then he would fall asleep while I went on staring
at the ceiling for hours, seeing nothing.

Sometimes I would walk slowly over to my bed while he stayed
seated on the old couch in the far corner, a book in his hands. He
would sit like that for hours. I'd toss from side to side, calling out
to him every few minutes. He'd answer me in a distracted voice,
and when he came over to go to sleep, I would caress him for a long
time. I reaped nothing but stolen glances that my only son cast our
way . . . until I saw him taking my son and leaving the house on many
occasions.

They went out together, came back together, and whenever I
asked him about it, he would say, "Don't be afraid. He is my son,
too, and my friend." And whenever I questioned my son, he would
look at me in astonishment . . . until the day came when he asked me,
"What do you want?"

He paused and then went on. "I am trying to see things as you
see them," he told me. "And he is trying to be a friend to me. All is
well and good. Let him give me some time so that I will know. To
this day I still cannot understand. Am I an Egyptian?"

And once, when we gathered at the supper table, I noticed my
son glancing at him as I served him food. I sensed the strange feel-
ings that passed through him as he confronted those glances.

When we were alone together, I began questioning him about
it again.

Do you know what he demanded of me today?" he asked me.
"What?"

"He told me he wants to have sex."

"No!" I shrieked, suddenly fearful. "No, don't help him do that!"
He shrugged. "Why not? He's grown up."

This was what I had dreaded—that my son would come to me
saying that he was about to leave. And that is exactly what happened,
a few days later.

"No," I said. "No," I said again.

But he paid no attention to me.

"I have no one left but you," I told him. "Your two brothers have
gone away, and only you are left!"

"I'm not the only one," he said. "You have him, too. He is of you,
and he's like you. But me? I'm not."

My third son went away, and now I was completely alone,
without anyone—not even him.

He comes to see me every evening and chats with me. He always
comes over, but that's all. We tell each other all sorts of things. I
recount every event of my day: I went to work, I came back, I met
many people, but there were others I didn't encounter. I went places
and said things, I heard stories, I laughed, I cried, I returned home.
I couldn't bear to stay there, so I went out again.

I walk in the streets, I sit in coffee shops, I smoke dope, I joke
with many men. I come home in the small hours of the night with
some of my friends, and we go on laughing and listening to strange
tales. When he comes in, he joins us, bantering until the first strands
of morning light appear. Then whoever wants to leave goes, and
whoever stays, stays, and falls asleep any old place. He sleeps beside
me as he does every night. Everyone thinks we're lovers, and they
say I'm his woman.

Every day it's the same thing, to the point where I get bored
sometimes and go away by myself to distant places. I return unal-
tered. But like all else, my sons have changed and are no longer as
they were.

Until that strange night . . . what happened? I don't know, but I
will tell you what I have learned of it and everything I was aware of
at the time.

New Year's Eve arrived. With it came a small group of friends, all carrying flasks. I had made some food, just snacks, and we began to gab and laugh and dance.

Not long before midnight, he came. He sat in a corner by himself and appeared not to see anyone. I was dancing with someone, but I noticed him watching me from his remote serenity. The looks he gave me were peaceful ones, but I sensed that they conveyed a great deal. A cheerful mood came over me and persisted. Yet it wasn't long before I felt weary.

The sad hour drew near, the hour of love and farewell. I left them all behind. I found myself going to him. I handed him his glass and kissed him. He kissed me and said nothing. He was becoming more and more withdrawn, ever more silent. My eyes on him, I began to drink. All I wanted was to keep drinking and to look at him.

Then it came back to me.

Crying, I tugged at his arm, for now I had remembered.

My children. They'd been here. I must show them to him. He must see them right at the stroke of twelve. I began to search for them everywhere, but I couldn't locate them.

"I just can't find them," I told him then. They were here, growing big in the sun, flourishing in the black earth. I used to set them down in the open, where there was a lot of room, in the clean, fresh air. People surrounded them with care. That is why they were healthy and strong. Here I made them grow. Their trunks grew. The sun tinted them and gave their faces color. In that other place, though, they took on a color like their father's, a color that was colorless.

I gaze at the places where they used to play. They have left me and gone away. I gave them everything, and so they took everything and went away and left me. They left me with nothing.

I loved them, and in all men I see them. Any man I meet might as well be my son, so I give him affection and want to hold him to myself. Yet all of the men misunderstand. All I want from them is love and an awareness of what I mean. I don't want money, I don't want protection, I don't want anything except love and understanding. But they misunderstand.

Just then the clock began to strike, counting the last few seconds. The sound of merrymaking arose among my friends, and the beating of the drums mounted inside my head. We all exchanged kisses, and together we opened our eyes upon the new moments.

After a little while, they began to leave, one after another, until they had all gone, and no one remained but me and him.

There is no one like my son, nor does my son resemble anyone. Tall and slender he is, and magnificent. He is beautiful and tyrannical and as hard and rough as solid rock. To my ear his voice is the sweetest of voices, and there is nothing like it. He averts his face from me and causes me pain. I cannot envelop him as I could on the day I got pregnant with him.

You, too—I carried you. I put you in my belly and suffered with you, enduring all the kinds of pain there are. Everything in you is him, but I am your woman. Come with me, and I will give you all you desire. Come, look how I can love you. I will pour your cup with my own hand; I will feed you until you have had your fill. And when you go to sleep, after I've let you taste of love, given you the sweetest taste that can be, I will cover you tenderly and give you warmth and stroke your head as I cradle it on my bosom. I know that no woman on earth will give to you as I do. Come, I will make a son out of you. I will make you a man like no man has ever been.

That night he bore me to the skies. He flew me away like a great angel circling through all the gardens of heaven. He had me taste all the fruits that I had been denied for years on end.[13] He sat with me on the banks of legendary rivers made of wine and sweet, fresh water. With his own hands he held the cup, and I drank the nectar of dates and of grapes. He showed me beautiful visions of the sweetest hues: apparitions of light, the angels of heaven, rosy cloud dreams. He touched me and took me in his arms and pressed me close, until I was a drink quenching his thirst and my own, and I grew like a seedling, dark green and alive.

In the morning he went away.

And afterward he came and went, staying away a lot. I declared that I would not open the door for him again, but he would show up, and I would open the door for him and hug him again and again. When he went away, I would weep, and every time, before he left, he would swear that he was mine. But after he'd gone, I would know he wasn't mine. This happened so many times that I wearied of counting them. I left my house and swore that when he returned he would not find me there. I stood on the riverbank for ages, and then I remembered that it was almost sunset and perhaps this evening he would come.

The sun vanished in the background, leaving behind only the dark red hue of the water and traces of color on the horizon. A car sped away from the river. I went on watching it until it disappeared and I could no longer see anything but the gray sky and the dirty, dusty buildings.

This is it: Cairo, the sad, elderly, city.

All it amounted to was that I did not want to go to the distant lands.

The faces of the children, like smothered flames, tortured me. Each day I screamed a thousand and one times and uttered a thousand and one curses on all of the things I had loved.

I did not want to go away. That's all. And now I know how dear staying on was and how much it cost me. I even cried out one night as I was wandering alone among the rocks: "Where is he? Where is God?"[14] But I wanted to stay, and I will go on wanting it, even if I have to wait for him every evening and he does not come, even if I spend all my time eyeing their possessions and furnishings, even if he does come one night and then goes away again while I look on from behind the lowered drapes.

Now my son is departing.

How unfortunate for me that I bore sons. How sad to be of them when not one of them is of me!

EASTWARD

I want to return the sun to its original place, whence it used to rise at the very beginning of creation, in the time when it gave light to the whole world and to the sky, and before the mighty giants came and flung it westward.

That day the coldness crept inside the ribs of the mountains. The pathways of the grieving earth were ruined. The huge yellow flowers hung their heads on their wilting necks and waited for the rain to come. The soft and tender songs slept on the lips of the river that goes on and on, never to return.

And the river comes forth from deep inside the earth.

We spend the night drinking and embracing each other and learning to walk. We lay our heads down on the ground, and it bends over us gently and tells us a story.

To learn how to walk, you must leave your cane behind.

Thus it was that the earth told us the tale.

Amm Ali said: I will tell you, my sons, the story of the last four days. But before I tell you the whole secret, I want to give you a clear picture of how I see things.

I view the world that surrounds me and see that it is a vast place, that it stretches as far as the four points of the compass reach. Its every expanse is marked by an endlessness the color of the rosy dawn, yet darkened by deep gray clouds.

Thus is the world.

And thus, at the crossroads, I see it. I have no choice before me but to follow one way, for the road goes on forever and does not return. Therefore, for each of the other three directions, there is one of three possibilities: the heart, the liver, the womb. As for the single seed that I keep with me, preserving it though I have no hope of fertility, I must send it eastward, and I must go with it.

On the first day, I knew that I would leave my heart to tackle the westward way, whence rise the odors of the ancient dust. I took my heart out of my chest, held it tightly in my hand, and entrusted it with my secrets, my earliest stories of love, and the archaic songs of maidens and youths. I suspended it at the front of the caravan heading west and charged the caravan leader to watch over it and give it the green liquid to drink whenever it began to shrink, until he would reach the highlands and find the dark and barren ground. Then he would search for my one and only love. When he found her, he would give my heart to her, that she might plant it in her hut once she had recrossed the Nile. Coming home in the evening from her daily voyage in the river's embrace, she would find that it had yielded a new bloom for her.

On the second day, I knew that I would send my liver northward, where the vast sea is. I tied it onto a small raft of waterskins and surrendered it to the peaceful river that was going north. On it I wrote my name, and I gave it my blessings and my hope that it would reach the sea, to scatter across the waters in tiny particles that would unite with all the sea's elements, evaporating with the water only to return to the sea with the rains.

As for the womb, I knew on the third day that I would carry it to the route going south. The great source there, perhaps, would make it fertile so that it would bring forth vegetation for the whole world. I gave it to the boatman to suspend on the tip of the sail so that the winds coming from the north would catch it and propel it toward the point whence the river comes. I bid the boatman, once there, to lay it in the bowels of the earth so that every year it would bring forth fruitful growth which would return with the river to the valley.

On the fourth day, I turned eastward carrying the single seed. I was filled with longing and hope that I would reach the land whence rises the sun. I knew I would encounter many terrors on the way, but my hopes were the more powerful. I packed my saddlebags, tossed my shirt over my shoulder, and rested my bundles on my back. When I got to my feet, I found that I was bent double. But I knew that after a few miles I would put down some of my burdens.[15] I did not know that I would pick up others, but that is what happened.

As I came to each alley, each street, I found something else that had been thrown aside or another tired person or another wounded animal, until I was no longer strong enough to go on. I sat down in a shaded corner and provisioned myself with some of the tales that I carried.

Amm Ali said: My one and only love told me a story on the morning of one of the Lord's days. The rose-colored rays were looking down over the sleeping world, and my love opened her eyes and looked at me and told me a story.

Amm Ali said: My one and only love said: With the color green, I wanted to write the letters of the heavens and the earth. But when I sat down to inscribe them, I discovered that they were all red, the color of a newborn rose. I put down my pen and swore to take them all in until I grew and stretched like a blossom of light.[16] I would unfold my body and arms, spreading my limbs around them, and plant my feet in the ground so their roots would reach down to the remotest depths. When I wanted to write—with the color green— the letters of the heavens and the earth, I dipped my pen in the new plants and drew the face of a person.

And this was enough.

At that moment I flung myself into the small boat and sailed to the other bank, for I wanted to reach the land whence rises the sun.

I walked along the sloping road, climbing up and down among the rocks. When I had gone one hundred cubits, I began to strip off all that encumbered me.

After another hundred cubits, I decided to strip off more, and after a third hundred, and a fourth and a fifth, I thought I would rid myself of everything before approaching the land whence rises the sun. When I was completely free of it all, I found myself raising my head, letting my hair fall loose, and running—snatching my arms from the darkness and running, my feet bare. From the fields I came, and to the far-flung sands I ran; and at the end of the road, I found the great tree that bears, each morning, a new sun.[17]

And the nearer I got, the taller my body grew and the more elongated it became. My toes and heels touched the ground with love and desire, and then, once again, they thrust forward into the air, swallowing new lengths, putting the ground behind them.

When I reached the great source of the river,[18] I washed myself in the sacred water. I continued on my way, the water dripping from my body and head, collecting to fall in large drops. Whenever a drop of water from my body touched the ground, blessed plants sprang up in its place.[19]

Amm Ali said: And thus I slept . . . and journeyed.

And this, I knew, was why God created the world.

NOTES

1. *Amm*   Literally, "paternal uncle." This form of address is used for older men to suggest affiliation, familiarity, and sometimes, affection. More generally, it is a mode of addressing older men who are perceived as having a similar or lower social status.

2. *"Go, dye yourself with henna," said the river, "for tomorrow you will be married."* This section draws on the legend of the Bride of the Nile. In ancient Egypt, each year a ceremony was held to ensure that the Nile would flood the next year and renew the farmland to each side. (See, further on: *"Perhaps it will come back to fertilize the earth as it once did."*) According to the author, it is not known whether the sacrifice thrown into the Nile was a human likeness or a human being. The practice continued through the Greek and Coptic periods, and recently there has been talk of reviving it for tourists.

3. *and he did not have enough time left to him* This passage is a story the author remembers hearing from her father when she was a child.

4. *on the bodice make a large sun* This passage evokes the dresses typical of Siwa Oasis in the Western Desert south of Marsa Matruh. However, the setting and the retelling, from a different perspective, of the Bride of the Nile legend suggest a Nilotic community, thus drawing together images from two divergent Egyptian societies.

5. *the story of the prince who crossed the seven seas* This echoes the "Maiden in the Tower" tales told to children by women. These often feature the folk figures al-Shatir Hasan and/or Sitt al-Husn (Clever Hasan and the Lady of Beauty). For related uses of children's tales in stories by contemporary Egyptian women writers, see Etidal Osman's "A House for Us" and Radwa Ashour's "Safsaafa and the General," in Marilyn Booth, ed. and trans., *Stories by Egyptian Women: My Grandmother's Cactus* (Austin, 1993).

6. *When the white thread of dawn clove the sky* This is one of a number of phrases in the story that echo Qur'anic diction. In the Qur'an (2:187), the believer is instructed to begin the daily fast during the month of Ramadan as soon as it is light enough that a white thread can be distinguished from "the black thread of the dawn." This and following translations follow M. M. Pickthall, *The Glorious Qur'an* (New York, 1984).

7. *it will bring me back, in a new life* The ancient Egyptians believed that after death they would follow the path of the sun into the west. Returning to life, they would recross the river to reach the eastern bank.

8. *carrying our dried stalks of wheat* This alludes to a harvest time practice. The first and finest ears of wheat are taken and braided into forms that are then hung on the doors of homes, inside where food is stored, in shop windows, and sometimes on piles of winnowed grain to insure abundant provision and a good crop next year. These ornaments are called `arusat al-qamh (the wheat bride or the wheat doll) and thus have a sort of metonymic terminological link to the events described at this point in the story.

The practice is described by Winifred Blackman in *The Fellahîn of Upper Egypt* (London, 1927), pp. 171–72. Blackman mentions that similar objects are found in ancient Egyptian tombs, pp. 307–8.

The author described the practice alluded to as a "Coptic practice." There are specifically Coptic practices of a similar nature, such as using dried cuttings from henna plants as good luck charms when they are hung in the four corners of a room and weaving palm fronds into decorations that are hung in a house to bring good luck. This is usually done around or after Easter, using the fronds from Palm Sunday (communication from Carol Bardenstein, February 1994).

9. *sitting in the eye of the sun, a crowned queen*   This is probably an allusion to the ancient Egyptian sky goddess, Nut, who was, among other appellations, called the "lady of Heliopolis" (in Arabic, `ayn al-shams, "eye of the sun") where worship of the sun was centered. See George Hart, *A Dictionary of Egyptian Gods and Goddesses* (London, 1986), p. 145. Thus, here, the sacrifice leads to a kind of immediate, visible, divinely constituted resurrection rather than to the victim's death.

10. *the only river that flows on steadily to the ends of the earth*   This may suggest the ancient Egyptian belief that a great sea surrounded the land, and the Nile was connected to it at both ends.

11. *dates both sweet and bitter*   The quintessential food of the desert. This also echoes words from the Qur'an.

12. *Mufida*   A given name, but the original meaning is "useful," "beneficial."

13. *taste all the fruits that I had been denied for years on end*   This paragraph echoes Qur'anic descriptions of heaven as a peaceful garden harboring fruit, greenness, streams of water where happiness reigns and regrets and fears are banished. Several times the Qur'an mentions a "garden of date palms and grapes." If these are earthly ones, suggesting the bounty of God's creation, still they bear echoes of the promised paradise (for example, see 2:66, 6:99, 17:91). Surat al-Nahl says: "[We give you to drink] of the fruits of the date palm, and grapes, whence you derive strong drink and good nourishment . . ." (16:67; see also 13:4, 16:11).

14. *I even cried out one night as I was wandering alone among the rocks: "Where is he? Where is God?*   This sentence was omitted from the originally published story because it suggested doubt in the existence of God; it has been added on advice from the author.

15. *after a few miles I would put down some of my burdens*   This also carries Qur'anic echoes. In 29:13 it is said that the unbelievers "will bear their own loads and other loads beside their own."

16. *until I grew and stretched like a blossom of light*   This image recalls Nut, ancient Egyptian goddess of the sky. She swallowed the sun each night and gave birth to it each morning. She is depicted as an elongated female, arms and feet outstretched perpendicular to her body, and her body is covered with stars. This seems both a protective and, literally, a supportive position, for Nut—who held up the sky—was sometimes visualized as a mother figure. She was believed to encompass the earth and hold the stars. Flower blossoms, particularly the lotus, were associated with the sun in ancient Egyptian mythology. (For more on Nut, see the Introduction to this collection.)

17. *the great tree that bears, each morning, a new sun*   There appears to be no specific equivalent to this in ancient Egyptian cosmology, but through the goddess Hathor—who was linked with the images of the tree and the cow—trees might come to have a symbolic link to fertility. Trees did have an association with nursing, from the symbolic association of the sycamore tree's white sap with milk (communication from Ann Roth, January 1994). The ritual importance of the sycamore tree and the linkage between trees and life/fertility remains

salient in Egyptian folk belief and narrative. (See Hasan El-Shamy, *Folktales of Egypt* [Chicago, 1980], p. 87.) The image here may be linked to that of Nut.

18.   *When I reached the great source of the river*   The Nile was thought by the ancients to originate where the world began, in a cave at Aswan.

19.   *blessed plants sprang up in its place*   The ancient Egyptian "Tale of the Two Brothers" is echoed in this motif. In that case, it was a tree that grew from the drops of blood from a slain bull who was, in fact, a young man in pursuit of his erstwhile wife. For a text of this story, whose details are too complex to give here, see Miriam Lichtheim, *Ancient Egyptian Literature,* vol. 2, *The New Kingdom* (Berkeley, 1976), pp. 203–11.

This passage also echoes the Greek legend of Adonis, who, when attacked by the ram-shaped Ares, bled to death. Wherever there fell a drop of his blood, the legend had it, anemones came up. Here the fluid is water rather than blood, perhaps the "water of life" found in folktales. But cf., in the Qur'an: "He has created humankind from a drop of fluid" (16:4).

THAT THE SUN MAY SINK

We were all circling about our own tiny patches and searching among our own things, alone. When we began to question each other, we found out that  we would all prefer to search for new land—green and fertile land—and men, and a sun that dead things would not eclipse. We knew then what we must do. We picked up our hoes and began to remove the heap. But after we had worked a long time, the hoes were falling to pieces, our bodies were sapped and thin, and we had not yet made any gain.

We were going away; the journey would take us far. We were cheerful, and everything seemed splendid. But when we were already a far piece down the road, it became clear that we had no choice but to return. And at that point, we had no recourse but silence. All that grieved me was that I had wanted to bring you the flower that you love, and it saddened me, too, that I was not able to tell you so when

Sahar Tawfiq, "An tanhadira al-shams," in *An tanhadira al-shams* (Cairo, 1985), pp. 97–107.

you asked your question. What had made me so sad, you asked as we returned from our journeying, from traveling halfway down the road.

All that happened was that I looked at you, many times. And every time I would revert and lower my eyes. I would know, as you gazed at a point somewhere in the distance, that if I were to speak I would say it all. And if I were to keep quiet, I would stifle it all. This is what will happen: I will go to the faraway edge and sit there looking at the two inclines that sink downward. I will let the breeze toy with me, and I will make a vow of renunciation to God to not think of this matter for a period of three days, or seven, or any number of days at all.

Then, ever so smoothly, resiliently, I am to return just as I left.

But even this I could not do. For when I went, terror and sadness befell me as I journeyed. So I could not do it, I said. In all the times that I went away, I did not squander this promise. I promised only that I would squander it the following time. On the last occasion, I inscribed a single word of plaint to God.

"You, O strange and severe illusion, what has brought you here a second time?"

The strange and severe illusion encompassed all things. I could not figure out how to escape from it, or to it. But I knew that it embraced the flowers, truth, love, the trees, gentleness, affection, the earth, and sex, and strange plants; that it included everything; and that I would have to overcome it, for otherwise I would be split in two, like the margins of a river, or I would sink with the sun.

As the sun was sinking, the earth raged. The river grew calm and gave itself over. But at precisely that place, which was where the sky came down to meet the land, the earth was roaring.

We were standing at the river's edge, watching the sun. When it was all over and nothing remained of the sun, we looked at each other, all of us, and fear and silence crept into our hearts. Just then our eyes were drawn to the sky, lit in the final instant by a thousand colors, as the river ran by, on and on, never losing its verve.

God is great, greater than the whole entire sky, greater than all things. God knows all things and dwells in all places.

Even there, atop the distant verge—when I go, no one is there, ever, not at any time, no one except me. Yet God dwells there.

Once the children were there, running and jumping and hiding behind the rocks, only to appear atop them, laughing. At that moment I stood far away, and I knew that now I could not do it, for the children owned everything, and no one could own them.

All it amounted to was that I had to bring the old things, all of them, with me. When I am in this place alone and only God is here and knows, I bury them. Each time I knew that he would ask me but that he would ask me with only a single glance. And he would avert his eyes from me, because he alone knew that now I was lying.

Lying—how hard it is to lie, harder than to do something that must be done when I'd like to do something else. And when it came to that, I would scream and scream and scream. Each time I screamed as never before. But even after that, I could not wrest out of myself that disheartening mass of terror and sudden alarm.

That day I went to him. I told him I was sorry, for I had lied, and I hoped fervently that he would forgive me. I told him I would lie again, only once more, or several times more. But I would come one day, I told him, and promise not to lie again.

I knew then that after today I would not be able to raise my eyes to his nor would I be able to promise anything, not even simply that I would go in his direction a second time.

Toward you, too, in your direction I cannot go. The blame, the bewilderment, the questioning to which I do not respond—no, I do not go in your direction, and you do not hear my screaming.

Today I see you, but my vision is not the same as on other days. You told me about the vast gardens and the sun. Every day there were vast gardens and sun. I used to see you there. But today things have changed. There, in the same small, cramped room, I really saw you. The sun did not pierce through to reach any of you as you sat there. Your own eyes looked like they never had before.

The strange man arrived on the difficult day. He built a house on top of the rise and took the earth and sky as his sheltering arbor. He gave commands and issued prohibitions and was obeyed. He erected iron railings along the roads and promised the new land to us. So we sat down, waiting. But all of you were going away, one after another, and you were not returning. When we asked about you, no one answered. We stood up and looked in every direction, all around us, toward every horizon, the strong light tiring our eyes. Time passed, and no one came back, and when we despaired, we sat down, waiting.

As for the strong sons of the earth, they had promised us other land, new land. It was run through with water moss and very salty, but it was ample, and it stretched all the way to the water. There, the savor of the air was sweet, untouched by bitterness or smoke.

The children cavorted around us and played and said, "We own the land." Many people went away to labor: to carry things, to gather firewood, to break up rocks. The children and the other men said, "We own the land." Men of great strength, they were birthed by the earth and the wild plants. "Come with us," they said. "We will cultivate the land with you, and we will await the ripe vegetation, the fruits." And so, then, I saw them, and I saw the crops thriving in the strong sunshine and growing tall. We carried water to the crops and protected them from the crows.

The time passed as we looked in all directions waiting for your return. When we despaired, we sat down, waiting. We looked toward the sun and waited for it to sink as it traveled to the end of the earth.

As the sun was sinking, the clouds and the edge of the sky were dipped in a severe and depressing tone, and the river surged, surged in a monotone, swallowing the very color in its own dark depths.

I stand in a difficult place. I await the moment of return. The earth craves water, for it is cracked and dry. I tread on the cracks, pressing down on them with my feet, and on the salt, the moss, the rough surface. The strange man came on the difficult day, his men arrayed up and down all the roads, their eyes on everyone.

I go among them. I come back. I bob up and down between them in play, and I laugh, and I'm torn to pieces. Their eyes are frozen, offering no response.

Three date palms rose over the hill. The children pointed to

them and chuckled. "The palm trees have taken root and grown big."
But we were sitting on the ground, in the dust, looking at them
without comprehension. "The palm trees have taken root and grown
big," they said.

I stand in a difficult place. I told you that I stand in a difficult
place. Yet I did not tell you everything because "everything" was also
full of difficulty. But when I looked at you, in the same instant, I
found that you knew, and so there was no longer anything new to
say.

But what exactly did happen right when the men arrived?

The men arrived riding on the back of the sun. The tireless sun
was coming right to the edge of the chasm. We had to get to our feet,
to get moving, but we waited for the sun to return with the coming
morning.

How shall we go to sleep and wake up when we have no inten-
tion of sleeping or waking?

In the nighttime and the darkness, the best thing to do was to
make love. It was a great thing to make love, but the unfortunate part
of it was that we had no idea what other things might be happening
in other places at the same moment.

When morning arrived, we looked at each other. No one knew
what had become visible on any of the others, but one thing had
become evident to all: we would have to begin, and now.

But I saw. Everything was brightly lit, and I saw. It was all clear
to me, clearer than it had to be. The most grievous error was that
I saw.

I looked at you, and I saw also that you knew and saw. I threw
down my hoe and ran far away from all of you. I went there—to the
same place, to the distant edge, the verge of the hill on which the
enormous structure rises. I looked at it, but then, turning back, I gave
a start, frightened. And it just so happened that I could not do it, for
the last time. One thing—after that day, I will never, ever return. I
said as much to the hill and the sky and to God, to everything there,
and I returned, gathering flowers on the way and breathing hard.

You, all of you, were standing there, listening to the story of the
men, the sons of the wild—the tale of the nomad who planted the

three palm trees. Looking at the trees was enough to make us feel that our chests were filled with fresh air. We were heading that way, searching for water, but the sun was passing the halfway point in the sky, and the green palm trees in the midst of the stretch of yellow were trembling in the wind. I looked at you, but you were going by, going on without a pause, your eyes glued to their fresh, young crowns.

Finally we walked toward the new land. It was cracked and dry, saturated with moss and salt; yet it was vast, unconfined, big enough to hold everyone and to suffice for their needs. They could work that land and pluck out the moss. To them it would yield fruit and the greenness of vegetation. We walked on, exploring its reaches, and, when we arrived at the three date palms, we found the water. Then we sat down to catch our breath and to look at the wide horizon.

The sun gives birth only to rays of light, and the rains deliver the earth and the verdure. The men give birth to silence, and the children bear love and the strength to act.

And the house erected there, on top of the hill, eclipses the sun. For that reason, we cast rocks at it. We run toward the sun, climb up over the rocks, talk to the sand and the ancient tombs, and we throw rocks at the house. The stones are ancient as the tombs; the sands are silent like the gray clouds at sunset, yet rumbling, surging, like the reddish clouds at the end of the earth.

And that strange man living there, in that very house erected atop the hill in order to eclipse the sun, he was lying. The lie was a very big one and a harsh one, and, when we saw the land that he had promised us, we knew without a doubt that he was lying. All the children had to know it, and they had to see it as we did—narrow and cramped, dark, barren, no houses nor people upon it, no love nor mercy.

The other land, promised to us by the strong men, the sons of the wild plants, was run through with moss and saltiness, but it was ample, and it stretched all the way to the water. There, the savor of the breeze was sweet, untouched by bitterness or smoke. There we put down our saddlebags, and we sat down on top of the rise. When the world grew dark, we clasped the children to our chests, for their heads drooped.

And as the sun was sinking, we could see it perfectly. But I knew, then, that I would definitely leave you there one day, go away alone, and sink with it.

THE TIME THAT IS NOT THIS

The walls of the dream
    collapsed
And opened onto a day that
    was yet stranger

I did not sleep during the night: for on this day, the riddling figures of the vision come to pass, and the forbidden door is opened. I step inside another land, steep my feet in the enchanted sea water. The amulets of my dream, I see, are forbidding the perils of those below to touch me, those who await the arrival of the horsemen coming from behind the portal.

I open my eyes and take in what lies before me: date palms that cast down a fruit I have not seen before and trees whose yield my fingers have never brushed. Except for that one tree—that tree, there was a time when it lived with me. I recognize it, but whence? I do not remember where or how or even in which time.

The walls of the dream collapsed
And opened onto a day that was yet stranger

Sahar Tawfiq, "Al-Zaman al-akhar," *Akhbar al-adab* (Cairo), no. 60 (September 1994): pp. 22–23.

Today we come out, emerging from behind bars that confined the horizon of vision. We walk through crowded ways—children and men, women whose heads are imprisoned, fast-moving buses, the clatter of a tram, the shouts of vendors, large signs showing their many colors between buildings of washed-out gray, streets saturated with dust.

Come, make your way with us, upward. We will come to another route on another day, for this day is but a dreary one, an austerity that bears no fruit. The trees that are still here have not been caught by the sun's rays, and so they have not put out leaves. Nor has the water of the Nile reached them. And so their arms have stretched out, reaching, searching for something else, something of which they are not aware, something that might rescue the cracked, split trunk and the confused roots, at a loss in the expanse of mute asphalt.

Make your way with us, upward. We will catch the tram that takes us far from home, exiles us. We will come away from a day that bears no fruit. Don't lag behind, don't try to stay, for this is the track of no return. Make your way with us, upward. Don't set your sights on those desert stretches that lay beyond the dusty buildings of death.

If you were to join us, we might stride toward the promised day in the land dream that perches hunched in a bewildered memory. We may open that door to the unknown. We may break through the wall of oblivion.

> The walls of the dream collapsed
> And opened onto a day that was yet stranger

Today we stand, untiring, in the bread line. The man selling bread hands it out; there is not enough. Folks count the loaves without really looking—counterfeit eyes in motionless sockets in faces faded to gray, saying nothing.

The brown loaves are few in number and limp. The line moves forward; we stand at the very end. When our turn finally comes, we take nothing. The bread has run out, and the vendor no longer has anything to offer us. The yellow coins in our hands no longer buy bread. What, then, is the use?

Do not despair. We will glimpse another track; we will find another route. The day that is not this will come. The time that is not this will be.

If it weren't for your failure to appear

If you had reached us in good time, we would not have had to go on waiting for you.

We stand at the head of the road, waiting, and the time passes, and a fear fills me, a dread of the far-flung maze of streets. We should have searched for you.

I press my way as quickly as I can along the jammed streets, every which way, shoving at the moving human effigies, eyes that are petrified, ears that do not hear, every figure carrying that meager bread close to the chest when I have no bread to carry.

I press on, my screams cleaving the confusion of sounds around me. I call you, I scream, my heart splits and rushes up into my throat, jetting out with my screams. I call out to you.

Children have come out of the belly of the earth to run before me, around me, ahead of me, to you.

And when you came
From within the dusty, faded, yellowish walls of death

The abrasions that resistance carves showed on your face and hands. Your grief gave me pain. The shattered looks that your eyes bore, a permanent question that they did not release, tormented me. This is my lot. My day has gone black, and I ache from the tears that your eyes have not released.

Come back to me.

Come, let us depart this strange day. Come, let us open the door of the dream that is forbidden; let us go out. We are coming to another world, a world that we know not.